CLASSICS OF SCIENCE FICTION AND FANTASY

Vol. 1, No. 3   February, 1971

I0628922

Cover by Bill Hughes, illustrating THE VALLEY OF SPIDERS.
Interiors by Christopher Hart, Bill Hughes, Eliot Keen, C. Durand
Chapman, Paul de Longpre and Leonard M. Davis.

EDITOR: Douglas Menville   ASSOC. EDITOR: R. Reginald

XCAVATIONS

AS I was browsing through a paperback book store the other day, a title that I had been hoping for years to see reprinted suddenly caught my eye. I was delighted, and eagerly grabbed a copy. The sales clerk, who knows my reading habits, raised an eyebrow and said, "Hey, I didn't know you liked westerns!"

"But this isn't just a western," I replied, "it's also a great fantasy novel that's been out of print for 25 years."

He gave me a funny look, as if he thought I was pulling his leg, but I wasn't.

The book was THE UNTAMED, by Max Brand (see "Calibrations" this issue). When it first appeared as a serial in 1918 in ALL-STORY WEEKLY, it was an immediate success, and hard-cover publication the following year started Max Brand on a career that made him one of the most popular western writers who ever lived. THE UNTAMED tells the story of a wild, savage man named Whistling Dan Barry, whose origin is unknown, whose strength and courage are phenomenal, and who seems to possess a supernatural control over animals. It is a beautifully written book, an exciting adventure story — and a fantasy. For Dan Barry is perhaps Pan himself, come to earth once more, struggling in mortal form to adjust to the restraints of civilization. The beauty of the writing is that we *feel* something alien about Dan Barry — but we are never sure.

Max Brand wrote a trilogy about Dan Barry: the other two books are THE NIGHT HORSEMAN (1920) and THE SEVENTH MAN (1921). After reading them, it is plainly evident why millions of people still read and collect the works of the man who probably wrote more words than any other writer who ever lived.

It is not generally known that Frederick Faust, the real name of the man who wrote as "Max Brand," along with a host of other pen-names, also wrote a number of excellent fantasy stories. Most of them are still buried in the pages of old magazines, but some have been reprinted over the years. The Dan Barry trilogy has been reprinted in paperback, but only THE UNTAMED is currently available. THE GARDEN OF EDEN, a strange novel of a hidden valley of mutant horses, appeared in paperback a few years ago. Several fantasy short stories were reprinted in FAMOUS FANTASTIC MYSTERIES and FANTASTIC NOVELS, and Faust's only long science fiction novel, THE SMOKING LAND, published under the name "George Challis," was reprinted in the February, 1950 issue of A. MERRITT'S FANTASY MAGAZINE. A complete discussion of Faust fantasy can be found in Darrell C. Richardson's fascinating book, MAX BRAND: THE MAN AND HIS WORK (Fantasy Publishing Co., Inc., 1952).

These stories are almost all of excellent quality, and definitely worthy of paperback reprinting, for unlike many pulp writers of the period, Max Brand could — and often did — write beautifully. Although he turned out over 25 million words during his lifetime, at heart he was a poet, and it was no accident that of all his published books, only three slim volumes of poetry bear the name "Frederick Faust."

DM

He had an impression of many eyes, of a dense crew of squat bodies . . .

THE VALLEY
OF
SPIDERS

by H. G. Wells

Illustrated by Christopher Hart

HERBERT GEORGE WELLS (1866 — 1946), along with Jules Verne, shares the distinction of being an amazing prophet and one of the founders of modern science fiction. Yet unlike Verne, who wrote mainly to entertain, Wells used science fiction and fantasy as vehicles to express his increasing outrage at the lack of political, social, and economic reforms in 20th-century society. He mercilessly attacked such injustices as the class structure, the repression of women, and the toleration of poverty and prejudice, and proposed a dream of a world ruled by reason and science. As he grew older, he saw his dream slip farther and farther away, and became more and more obsessed with the problems of the world. His literary output reflected these obsessions to the degree that his later novels became mere preachments, almost totally devoid of literary merit. He lived to see the direst of his prophecies come true, in spite of his many warnings: World War II, the fearful air battles he predicted in THE WAR IN THE AIR (1908), and the atomic bomb he foresaw in THE WORLD SET FREE (1914). But Wells is chiefly remembered for his excellent early science fiction and fantasy novels (THE TIME MACHINE, THE WAR OF THE WORLDS, THE FIRST MEN IN THE MOON, THE INVISIBLE MAN, and many others) and short stories, most of which appeared in popular magazines of the late 1800's and early 1900's. "The Valley of Spiders" is a strange, off-trail story, quite different from most of Wells' other works. It is the closest he ever came to adventure fantasy, and appeared in his 1903 collection, TWELVE STORIES AND A DREAM.

TOWARDS midday the three pursuers came abruptly round a bend in the torrent bed upon the sight of a very broad and spacious valley. The difficult and winding trench of pebbles along which they had tracked the fugitives for so long expanded to a broad slope, and with a common impulse the three men left the trail, and rode to a little eminence set with olive-dun trees, and there halted, the two others, as became them, a little behind the man with the silver-studded bridle.

For a space they scanned the great expanse below them with eager eyes. It spread remoter and remoter, with only a few clusters of sere thorn bushes here and there, and the dim suggestions of some now waterless ravine to break its desolation of yellow grass. Its purple distances melted at last into the bluish slopes of the further hills — hills it might be of a greener kind — and above them, invisibly supported, and seeming indeed to hang in the blue, were the snow-clad summits of mountains — that grew larger and bolder to the north-westward as the sides of the valley drew together. And westward the valley opened until a distant darkness under the sky told where the forests began. But the three men looked neither east nor west, but only steadfastly across the valley.

The gaunt man with the scarred lip was the first to speak. "Nowhere," he said, with a sigh of disappointment in his voice. "But after all, they had a full day's start."

"They don't know we are after them," said the little man on the white horse.

"*She* would know," said the leader bitterly, as if speaking to himself.

"Even then they can't go fast. They've got no beast but the mule, and all to-day the girl's foot has been bleeding —"

The man with the silver bridle flashed a quick intensity of rage on him. "Do you think I haven't seen that?" he snarled.

"It helps, anyhow," whispered the little man to himself.

The gaunt man with the scarred lip stared impassively. "They can't be over the valley," he said. "If we ride hard —"

He glanced at the white horse and paused.

"Curse all white horses!" said the man with the silver bridle, and turned to scan the beast his curse included.

The little man looked down between the melancholy ears of his steed.

"I did my best," he said.

The two others stared again across the valley for a space. The gaunt man passed the back of his hand across the scarred lip.

"Come up!" said the man who owned the silver bridle, suddenly. The little man started and jerked his rein, and the horse hoofs of the three made a multitudinous faint pattering upon the withered grass as they turned back towards the trail. . . .

They rode cautiously down the long slope before them, and

so came through a waste of prickly twisted bushes and strange dry shapes of thorny branches that grew amongst the rocks, into the levels below. And there the trail grew faint, for the soil was scanty, and the only herbage was this scorched dead straw that lay upon the ground. Still, by hard scanning, by leaning beside the horses' necks and pausing ever and again, even these white men could contrive to follow after their prey.

There were trodden places, bent and broken blades of the coarse grass, and ever and again the sufficient intimation of a footmark. And once the leader saw a brown smear of blood where the half-caste girl may have trod. And at that under his breath he cursed her for a fool.

The gaunt man checked his leader's tracking, and the little man on the white horse rode behind, a man lost in a dream. They rode one after another, the man with the silver bridle led the way, and they spoke never a word.

After a time it came to the little man on the white horse that the world was very still. He started out of his dream. Besides the little noises of their horses and equipment, the whole great valley kept the brooding quite of a painted scene.

Before him went his master and his fellow, each intently leaning forward to the left, each impassively moving with the paces of his horse; their shadows went before them — still, noiseless, tapering attendants; and nearer a crouched cool shape was his own. He looked about him. What was it had gone? Then he remembered the reverberation from the banks of the gorge and the perpetual accompaniment of shifting, jostling pebbles. And, moreover —? There was no breeze. That was it! What a vast, still place it was, a monotonous afternoon slumber! And the sky open and blank except for a sombre veil of haze that had gathered in the upper valley.

He straightened his back, fretted with his bridle, puckered his lips to whistle, and simply sighed. He turned in his saddle for a time, and stared at the throat of the mountain gorge out of which they had come. Blank! Blank slopes on either side, with never a sign of a decent beast or tree — much less a man. What a land it was! What a wilderness! He dropped again into his former pose.

It filled him with a momentary pleasure to see a wry stick of purple black flash out into the form of a snake, and vanish amidst the brown. After all, the infernal valley *was* alive. And then, to rejoice him still more, came a little breath across his face, a whisper that came and went, the faintest inclination of a stiff black-antlered bush upon a little crest, the first intimations of a possible breeze. Idly he wetted his finger and held it up.

He pulled up sharply to avoid a collision with the gaunt man, who had stopped at fault upon the trail. Just at that guilty moment he caught his master's eye looking towards him.

For a time he forced an interest in the tracking. Then, as they rode on again, he studied his master's shadow and hat and shoulder, appearing and disappearing behind the gaunt man's nearer contours. They had ridden four days out of the very limits of the world into this desolate place, short of water, with nothing but a strip of dried meat under their saddles, over rocks and mountains, where surely none but these fugitives had ever been before — for *that!*

And all this was for a girl, a mere wilful child! And the man had whole cityfuls of people to do his basest bidding — girls, women! Why in the name of passionate folly *this* one in particular? asked the little man, and scowled at the world, and licked his parched lips with a blackened tongue. It was the way of the master, and that was all he knew. Just because she sought to evade him . . .

His eye caught a whole row of high-plumed canes bending in unison, and then the tails of silk that hung before his neck flapped and fell. The breeze was growing stronger. Somehow it took the stiff stillness out of things — and that was well.

"Hallo!" said the gaunt man.

All three stopped abruptly.

"What?" asked the master. "What?"

"Over there," said the gaunt man, pointing up the valley.

"What?"

"Something coming towards us."

And as he spoke a yellow animal crested a rise and came bearing down upon them. It was a big wild dog, coming before the wind, tongue out, at a steady pace, and running with such an intensity of purpose that he did not seem to see the horsemen he approached. He ran with his nose up, following, it was plain, neither scent nor quarry. As he drew nearer the little man felt for his sword. "He's mad," said the gaunt rider.

"Shout!" said the little man, and shouted.

The dog came on. Then when the little man's blade was

already out, it swerved aside and went panting by them and passed. The eyes of the little man followed its flight. "There was no foam," he said. For a space the man with the silver-studded bridle stared up the valley. "Oh, come on!" he cried at last. "What does it matter?" and jerked his horse into movement again.

The little man left the insoluble mystery of a dog that fled from nothing but the wind, and lapsed into profound musings on human character. "Come on!" he whispered to himself. "Why should it be given to one man to say 'Come on!' with that stupendous violence of effect? Always, all his life, the man with the silver bridle has been saying that. If *I* said it —!" thought the little man. But people marvelled when the master was disobeyed even in the wildest things. This half-caste girl seemed to him, seemed to every one, mad — blasphemous almost. The little man, by way of comparison, reflected on the gaunt rider with the scarred lip, as stalwart as his master, as brave and, indeed, perhaps braver, and yet for him there was obedience, nothing but to give obedience duly and stoutly....

Certain sensations of the hands and knees called the little man back to more immediate things. He became aware of something. He rode up beside his gaunt fellow. "Do you notice the horses?" he said in an undertone.

The gaunt face looked interrogation.

"They don't like this wind," said the little man, and dropped behind as the man with the silver bridle turned upon him.

"It's all right," said the gaunt-faced man.

They rode on again for a space in silence. The foremost two rode downcast upon the trail, the hindmost man watched the haze that crept down the vastness of the valley, nearer and nearer, and noted how the wind grew in strength moment by moment. Far away on the left he saw a line of dark bulks — wild hog, perhaps, galloping down the valley, but of that he said nothing, nor did he remark again upon the uneasiness of the horses.

And then he saw first one and then a second great white ball, a great shining white ball like a gigantic head of thistledown, that drove before the wind athwart the path. These balls soared high in the air, and dropped and rose again and caught for a moment, and hurried on and passed, but at the sight of them the restlessness of the horses increased.

Then presently he saw that more of these drifting globes —
and then soon very many more — were hurrying towards him
down the valley.

They became aware of a squealing. Athwart the path a huge
boar rushed, turned his head but for one instant to glance at
them, and then hurling on down the valley again. And at that all
three stopped and sat in their saddles, staring into the
thickening haze that was coming upon them.

"If it were not for this thistledown —" began the leader.

But now a big globe came drifting past within a score of
yards of them. It was really not an even sphere at all, but a vast,
soft, ragged, filmy thing, a sheet gathered by the corners, an
aerial jelly-fish, as it were, but rolling over and over as it
advanced, and trailing long cob-webby threads and streamers
that floated in its wake.

"It isn't thistledown," said the little man.

"I don't like the stuff," said the gaunt man.

And they looked at one another.

"Curse it!" cried the leader. "The air's full of it up there. If it
keeps on at this pace long, it will stop us altogether."

An instinctive feeling, such as lines out a herd of deer at the
approach of some ambiguous thing, prompted them to turn
their horses to the wind, ride forward a few paces, and stare at
that advancing multitude of floating masses. They came on
before the wind with a sort of smooth swiftness, rising and
falling noiselessly, sinking to earth, rebounding high, soaring —
all with a perfect unanimity, with a still, deliberate assurance.

Right and left of the horsemen the pioneers of this strange
army passed. At one that rolled along the ground, breaking
shapelessly and trailing out reluctantly into long grappling
ribbons and bands, all three horses began to shy and dance. The
master was seized with a sudden, unreasonable impatience. He
cursed the drifting globes roundly. "Get on!" he cried; "get on!
What do these things matter? How *can* they matter? Back to the
trail!" He fell swearing at his horse and sawed the bit across its
mouth.

He shouted aloud with rage. "I will follow that trail, I tell
you," he cried. "Where is the trail?"

He gripped the bridle of his prancing horse and searched
amidst the grass. A long and clinging thread fell across his face,
a grey streamer dropped about his bridle arm, some big, active

thing with many legs ran down the back of his head. He looked up to discover one of those grey masses anchored as it were above him by these things and flapping out ends as a sail flaps when a boat comes about — but noiselessly.

He had an impression of many eyes, of a dense crew of squat bodies, of long, many-jointed limbs hauling at their mooring ropes to bring the thing down upon him. For a space he stared up, reining in his prancing horse with the instinct born of years of horsemanship. Then the flat of a sword smote his back, and a blade flashed overhead and cut the drifting balloon of spider-web free, and the whole mass lifted softly and drove clear and away.

"Spiders!" cried the voice of the gaunt man. "The things are full of big spiders! Look, my lord!"

The man with the silver bridle still followed the mass that drove away.

"Look, my lord!"

The master found himself staring down at a red smashed thing on the ground that, in spite of partial obliteration, could still wriggle unavailing legs. Then, when the gaunt man pointed to another mass that bore down upon them, he drew his sword hastily. Up the valley now it was like a fog bank torn to rags. He tried to grasp the situation.

"Ride for it!" the little man was shouting. "Ride for it down the valley."

What happened then was like the confusion of a battle. The man with the silver bridle saw the little man go past him, slashing furiously at imaginary cobwebs, saw him cannon into the horse of the gaunt man and hurl it and its rider to earth. His own horse went a dozen paces before he could rein it in. Then he looked up to avoid imaginary dangers, and then back again to see a horse rolling on the ground, the gaunt man standing and slashing over it at a rent and fluttering mass of grey that streamed and wrapped about them both. And thick and fast as thistledown on waste land on a windy day in July the cobweb masses were coming on.

The little man had dismounted, but he dared not release his horse. He was endeavouring to lug the struggling brute back with the strength of one arm, while with the other he slashed aimlessly. The tentacles of a second grey mass had entangled themselves with the struggle, and this second grey mass came to its moorings, and slowly sank.

The master set his teeth, gripped his bridle, lowered his head, and spurred his horse forward. The horse on the ground rolled over, there was blood and moving shapes upon the flanks, and the gaunt man suddenly leaving it, ran forward towards his master, perhaps ten paces. His legs were swathed and encumbered with grey; he made ineffectual movements with his sword. Grey streamers waved from him; there was a thin grey veil across his face. With his left hand he beat at something on his body, and suddenly he stumbled and fell. He struggled to rise, and fell again and suddenly, horribly, began to howl, "Oh — ohoo, ohooh!"

The master could see the great spiders upon him, and others upon the ground.

As he strove to force his horse nearer to this gesticulating, screaming grey object that struggled up and down, there came a clatter of hoofs, and the little man, in the act of mounting, swordless, balanced on his belly athwart the white horse, and clutching its mane, whirled past. And again a clinging thread of grey gossamer swept across the master's face. All about him, and over him, it seemed this drifting, noiseless cobweb circled and drew near him. . . .

To the day of his death he never knew just how the event of that moment happened. Did he, indeed, turn his horse, or did it really of its own accord stampede after its fellow? Suffice it that in another second he was galloping full tilt down the valley with his sword whirling furiously overhead. And all about him on the quickening breeze, the spiders' air-ships, their air bundles and air sheets, seemed to him to hurry in a conscious pursuit.

Clatter, clatter, thud, thud — the man with the silver bridle rode, heedless of his direction, with his fearful face looking up now right, now left, and his sword arm ready to slash. And a few hundred yards ahead of him, with a trail of torn cobweb trailing behind him, rode the little man on the white horse, still but imperfectly in the saddle. The reeds bent before them, the wind blew fresh and strong, over his shoulder the master could see the webs hurrying to overtake. . . .

He was so intent to escape the spiders' webs that only as his horse gathered together for a leap did he realise the ravine ahead. And then he realised it only to misunderstand and interfere. He was leaning forward on his horse's neck and sat up and back all too late.

But if in his excitement he had failed to leap, at any rate he had not forgotten how to fall. He was horseman again in mid-air. He came off clear with a mere bruise upon his shoulder, and his horse rolled, kicking spasmodic legs, and lay still. But the master's sword drove its point into the hard soil, and snapped clean across, as though Chance refused him any longer as her Knight, and the splintered end missed his face by an inch or so.

He was on his feet in a moment, breathlessly scanning the on-rushing spider-webs. For a moment he was minded to run, and then thought of the ravine, and turned back. He ran aside once to dodge one drifting terror, and then he was swiftly clambering down the precipitous sides, and out of the touch of the gale.

There, under the lee of the dry torrent's steeper banks, he might crouch and watch these strange, grey masses pass and pass in safety till the wind fell, and it became possible to escape. And there for a long time he crouched, watching the strange, grey, ragged masses trail their streamers across his narrowed sky.

Once a stray spider fell into the ravine close beside him — a full foot it measured from leg to leg and its body was half a man's hand — and after he had watched its monstrous alacrity of search and escape for a little while and tempted it to bite his broken sword, he lifted up his iron-heeled boot and smashed it into a pulp. He swore as he did so, and for a time sought up and down for another.

Then presently, when he was surer these spider swarms could not drop into the ravine, he found a place where he could sit down, and sat and fell into deep thought and began, after his manner, to gnaw his knuckles and bite his nails. And from this he was moved by the coming of the man with the white horse.

He heard him long before he saw him, as a clattering of hoofs, stumbling footsteps, and a reassuring voice. Then the little man appeared, a rueful figure, still with a tail of white cobweb trailing behind him. They approached each other without speaking, without a salutation. The little man was fatigued and shamed to the pitch of hopeless bitterness, and came to a stop at last, face to face with his seated master. The latter winced a little under his dependent's eye. "Well?" he said at last, with no pretence of authority.

"You left him?"

"My horse bolted."

"I know. So did mine."

He laughed at his master mirthlessly.

"I say my horse bolted," said the man who once had a silver-studded bridle.

"Cowards both," said the little man.

The other gnawed his knuckle through some meditative moments, with his eye on his inferior.

"Don't call me a coward," he said at length.

"You are a coward, like myself."

"A coward possibly. There is a limit beyond which every man must fear. That I have learnt at last. But not like yourself. That is where the difference comes in."

"I never could have dreamt you would have left him. He saved your life two minutes before . . . Why are you our lord?"

The master gnawed his knuckles again, and his countenance was dark.

"No man calls me a coward," he said. "No. . . . A broken sword is better than none. . . . One spavined white horse cannot be expected to carry two men a four days' journey. I hate white horses, but this time it cannot be helped. You begin to understand me? I perceive that you are minded, on the strength of what you have seen and fancy, to taint my reputation. It is men of your sort who unmake kings. Besides which — I never liked you."

"My lord!" said the little man.

"No," said the master. *"No!"*

He stood up sharply as the little man moved. For a minute perhaps they faced one another. Overhead the spiders' balls went driving. There was a quick movement among the pebbles; a running of feet, a cry of despair, a gasp and a blow. . . .

Towards nightfall the wind fell. The sun set in a calm serenity, and the man who had once possessed the silver bridle came at last very cautiously and by an easy slope out of the ravine again; but now he led the white horse that once belonged to the little man. He would have gone back to his horse to get his silver-mounted bridle again, but he feared night and a quickening breeze might still find him in the valley, and besides, he disliked greatly to think he might discover his horse all swathed in cobwebs and perhaps unpleasantly eaten.

And as he thought of those cobwebs, and of all the dangers he had been through, and the manner in which he had been preserved that day, his hand sought a little reliquary that hung about his neck, and he clasped it for a moment with heartfelt gratitude. As he did so his eyes went across the valley.

"I was hot with passion," he said, "and now she has met her reward. They also, no doubt —"

And behold! far away out of the wooded slopes across the valley, but in the clearness of the sunset, distinct and unmistakable, he saw a little spire of smoke.

At that his expression of serene resignation changed to an amazed anger. Smoke? He turned the head of the white horse about, and hesitated. And as he did so a little rustle of air went through the grass about him. Far away upon some reeds swayed a tattered sheet of grey. He looked at the cobwebs; he looked at the smoke.

"Perhaps, after all, it is not them," he said at last.

But he knew better.

After he had stared at the smoke for some time, he mounted the white horse.

As he rode, he picked his way amidst stranded masses of web. For some reason there were many dead spiders on the ground, and those that lived feasted guiltily on their fellows. At the sound of his horse's hoofs they fled.

Their time had passed. From the ground, without either a wind to carry them or a winding-sheet ready, these things, for all their poison, could do him little evil.

He flicked with his belt at those he fancied came too near. Once, where a number ran together over a bare place, he was minded to dismount and trample them with his boots, but this impulse he overcame. Ever and again he turned in his saddle, and looked back at the smoke.

"Spiders," he muttered over and over again. "Spiders. Well, well . . . The next time I must spin a web."

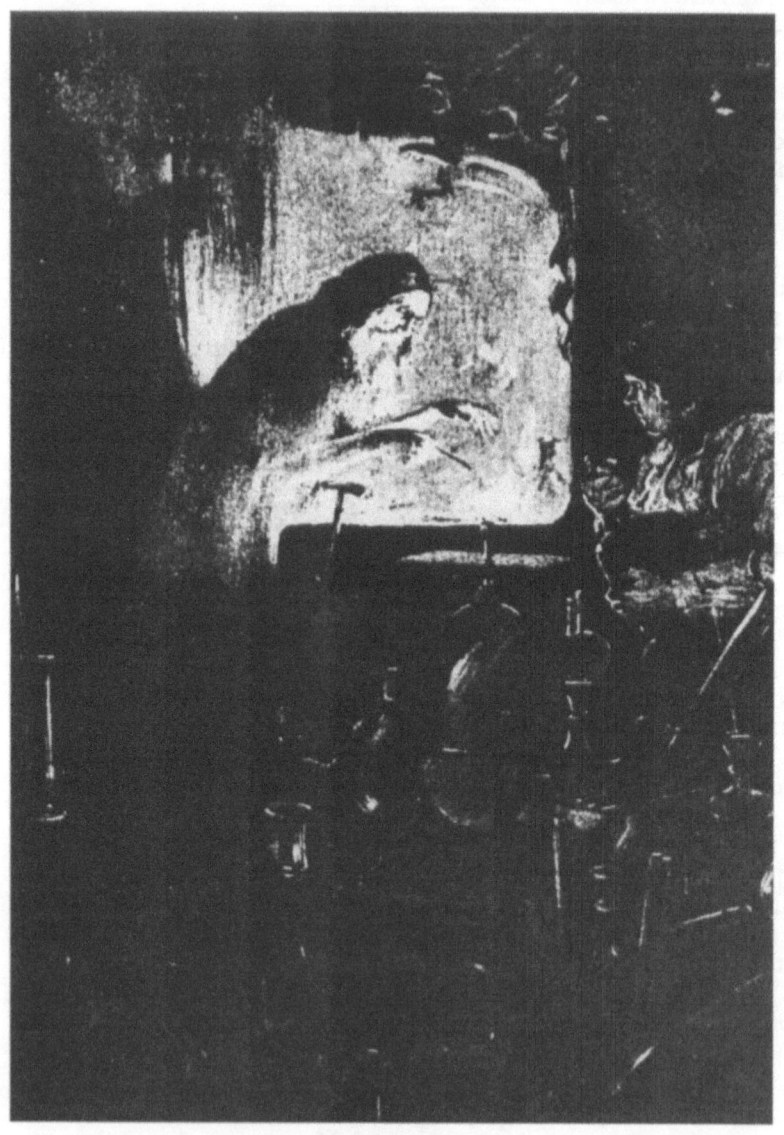

He was pale as death, anxious and absorbed . . .

THE BIRTHMARK

by Nathaniel Hawthorne

Illustrated by Eliot Keen

NATHANIEL HAWTHORNE (1804 — 1864), a writer whose work has profoundly influenced the course of American literature, was the descendant of John Hathorne, one of the judges in the infamous Salem Witchcraft Trials of the 1600's. Hathorne and all his descendants were cursed by one of his victims, a fact which shamed and frightened the Hathorne family for over two hundred years. Even in Nathaniel's day the curse was taken seriously, and the author himself added a "w" to the family name, perhaps in an attempt to mislead supernatural retribution. After a stern and gloomy childhood, Hawthorne graduated from Bowdoin College in 1825, a classmate of Henry Wadsworth Longfellow and Franklin Pierce, who later became our fourteenth President. Hawthorne settled in Salem, where he began writing tales and sketches for magazines, newspapers, and gift annuals, mostly anonymously. He was moody and reticent, plagued with self-doubt and obsessed with the concept of sin and its relation to his Puritan background, a theme which pervades all his later work. With the publication of his first book of stories in 1837, TWICE-TOLD TALES, Hawthorne began to win for himself a small but appreciative audience. After an unpleasant experience with the experimental Brook Farm community in 1841, he left to resume writing, and in 1842 married Sophia Peabody. Their son, Julian Hawthorne, was born in 1846 and became a writer of note himself, composing, among other essays, a long and laudatory preface to THE GODDESS OF ATVATABAR! Publication of THE SCARLET LETTER in 1850 made Nathaniel Hawthorne famous and financially independent at last, and was followed by such well-known works as THE HOUSE OF THE SEVEN GABLES (1851); THE SNOW IMAGE AND OTHER TALES (1851); THE BLITHEDALE ROMANCE (1852), based on his Brook Farm experiences; and THE MARBLE FAUN (1860). Many of Hawthorne's stories are allegories and outright fantasies, and others contain fantastic elements, but only three or four can be classed as science fiction. Yet Hawthorne was

keenly interested in the scientific knowledge of his day, and the following
tale powerfully demonstrates the "sin" of the scientist who loses touch
with humanity by making science a religion, later to become one of the
classic themes of twentieth-century science fiction. "The Birthmark" first
appeared in THE PIONEER magazine in 1843, and was later included in
MOSSES FROM AN OLD MANSE (1846).

IN the latter part of the last century, there lived a man of
science, an eminent proficient in every branch of natural
philosophy, who not long before our story opens had made
experience of a spiritual affinity more attractive than any
chemical one. He had left his laboratory to the care of an
assistant, cleared his fine countenance from the furnace smoke,
washed the stain of acids from his fingers, and persuaded a
beautiful woman to become his wife. In those days when the
comparatively recent discovery of electricity and other kindred
mysteries of Nature seemed to open paths into the region of
miracle, it was not unusual for the love of science to rival the
love of woman in its depth and absorbing energy. The higher
intellect, the imagination, the spirit, and even the heart might
all find their congenial aliment in pursuits which, as some of
their ardent votaries believed, would ascend from one step of
powerful intelligence to another, until the philosopher should
lay his hand on the secret of creative force and perhaps make
new worlds for himself. We know not whether Aylmer
possessed this degree of faith in man's ultimate control over
Nature. He had devoted himself, however, too unreservedly to
scientific studies ever to be weaned from them by any second
passion. His love for his young wife might prove the stronger of
the two; but it could only be by intertwining itself with his love
of science, and uniting the strength of the latter to his own.

Such a union accordingly took place, and was attended with
truly remarkable consequences and a deeply impressive moral.
One day, very soon after their marriage, Aylmer sat gazing at his
wife with a trouble in his countenance that grew stronger until
he spoke.

"Georgiana," said he, "has it never occurred to you that the
mark upon your cheek might be removed?"

"No, indeed," said she, smiling; but perceiving the seriousness
of his manner, she blushed deeply. "To tell you the truth, it has
been so often called a charm that I was simple enough to
imagine it might be so."

"Ah, upon another face perhaps it might," replied her husband, "but never on yours. No, dearest Georgiana, you came so nearly perfect from the hand of Nature that this slightest possible defect, which we hesitate whether to term a defect or a beauty, shocks me, as being the visible mark of earthly imperfection."

"Shocks you, my husband!" cried Georgiana, deeply hurt; at first reddening with momentary anger, but then bursting into tears. "Then why did you take me from my mother's side? You cannot love what shocks you!"

To explain this conversation, it must be mentioned that in the center of Georgiana's left cheek there was a singular mark, deeply interwoven, as it were, with the texture and substance of her face. In the usual state of her complexion — a healthy though delicate bloom — the mark wore a tint of deeper crimson, which imperfectly defined its shape amid the surrounding rosiness. When she blushed, it gradually became more indistinct, and finally vanished amid the triumphant rush of blood that bathed the whole cheek with its brilliant glow. But if any shifting motion caused her to turn pale, there was the mark again, a crimson stain upon the snow, in what Aylmer sometimes deemed an almost fearful distinctness. Its shape bore not a little similarity to the human hand, though of the smallest pygmy size. Georgiana's lovers were wont to say that some fairy at her birth hour had laid her tiny hand upon the infant's cheek, and left this impress there in token of the magic endowments that were to give her such sway over all hearts. Many a desperate swain would have risked life for the privilege of pressing his lips to the mysterious hand. It must not be concealed, however, that the impression wrought by this fairy sign manual varied exceedingly, according to the difference of temperament in the beholders. Some fastidious persons — but they were exclusively of her own sex — affirmed that the bloody hand, as they chose to call it, quite destroyed the effect of Georgiana's beauty, and rendered her countenance even hideous. But it would be as reasonable to say that one of those small blue stains which sometimes occur in the purest statuary marble would convert the Eve of Powers to a monster. Masculine observers, if the birthmark did not heighten their admiration, contended themselves with wishing it away, that the world might possess one living specimen of ideal loveliness without the semblance of a flaw. After his marriage — for he thought little or nothing of the matter before — Aylmer discovered that this was the case with himself.

Had she been less beautiful — if Envy's self could have found aught else to sneer at — he might have felt his affection heightened by the prettiness of this mimic hand, now vaguely portrayed, now lost, now stealing forth again and glimmering to and fro with every pulse of emotion that throbbed within her heart; but seeing her otherwise so perfect, he found this one defect grow more and more intolerable with every moment of their united lives. It was the fatal flaw of humanity which Nature, in one shape or another, stamps ineffaceably on all her productions, either to imply that they are temporary and finite, or that their perfection must be wrought by toil and pain. The crimson hand expressed the ineludible grip in which mortality clutches the highest and purest of earthly mold, degrading them into kindred with the lowest, and even with the very brutes, like whom their visible frames return to dust. In this manner, selecting it as the symbol of his wife's liability to sin, sorrow, decay, and death, Aylmer's somber imagination was not long in rendering the birthmark a frightful object, causing him more trouble and horror than ever Georgiana's beauty, whether of soul or sense, had given him delight.

At all the seasons which should have been their happiest, he invariably and without intending it, nay, in spite of a purpose to the contrary, reverted to this one disastrous topic. Trifling as it at first appeared, it so connected itself with innumerable trains of thought and modes of feeling that it became the central point of all. With the morning twilight, Aylmer opened his eyes upon his wife's face and recognized the symbol of imperfection; and when they sat together at the evening hearth, his eyes wandered stealthily to her cheek, and beheld, flickering with the blaze of the wood fire, the spectral hand that wrote mortality where he would fain have worshiped. Georgiana soon learned to shudder at his gaze. It needed but a glance with the peculiar expression that his face often wore to change the roses of her cheek into a deathlike paleness, amid which the crimson hand was brought strongly out, like a bas-relief of ruby on the whitest marble.

Late one night, when the lights were growing dim, so as hardly to betray the stain on the poor wife's cheek, she herself, for the first time, voluntarily took up the subject.

"Do you remember, my dear Aylmer," said she, with a feeble attempt at a smile, "have you any recollection of a dream last night about this odious hand?"

"None! none whatever!" replied Aylmer, starting; but then he added, in a dry, cold tone, affected for the sake of concealing the real depth of his emotion, "I might well dream of it; for before I fell asleep it had taken a pretty firm hold of my fancy."

"And you did dream of it?" continued Georgiana, hastily; for she dreaded lest a gush of tears should interrupt what she had to say. "A terrible dream! I wonder that you can forget it. Is it possible to forget this one expression? — 'It is in her heart now; we must have it out!' Reflect, my husband; for by all means I would have you recall that dream."

The mind is in a sad state when Sleep, the all-involving, cannot confine her specters within the dim region of her sway, but suffers them to break forth, affrighting this actual life with secrets that perchance belong to a deeper one. Aylmer now remembered his dream. He had fancied himself with his servant Aminadab, attempting an operation for the removal of the birthmark; but the deeper went the knife, the deeper sank the hand, until at length its tiny grasp appeared to have caught hold of Georgiana's heart; whence, however, her husband was inexorably resolved to cut or wrench it away.

When the dream had shaped itself perfectly in his memory, Aylmer sat in his wife's presence with a guilty feeling. Truth often finds its way to the mind close muffled in robes of sleep, and then speaks with uncompromising directness of matters in regard to which we practice an unconscious self-deception during our waking moments. Until now he had not been aware of the tyrannizing influence acquired by one idea over his mind, and of the lengths which he might find in his heart to go for the sake of giving himself peace.

"Aylmer," resumed Georgiana, solemnly, "I know not what may be the cost to both of us to rid me of this fatal birthmark. Perhaps its removal may cause cureless deformity; or it may be the stain goes as deep as life itself. Again, do we know that there is a possibility, on any terms, of unclasping the firm grip of this little hand which was laid upon me before I came into the world?"

"Dearest Georgiana, I have spent much thought upon the subject," hastily interrupted Aylmer. "I am convinced of the perfect practicability of its removal."

"If there be the remotest possibility of it," continued Georgiana, "let the attempt be made at whatever risk. Danger is nothing to me; for life, while this hateful mark makes me the object of your horror and disgust — life is a burden which I would fling down with joy. Either remove this dreadful hand, or take my wretched life! You have deep science. All the world bears witness of it. You have achieved great wonders. Cannot you remove this little, little mark, which I cover with the tips of two small fingers? Is this beyond your power, for the sake of your own peace, and to save your poor wife from madness?"

"Noblest, dearest, tenderest wife," cried Aylmer, rapturously, "doubt not my power. I have already given this matter the deepest thought — thought which might almost have enlightened me to create a being less perfect than yourself. Georgiana, you have led me deeper than ever into the heart of science. I feel myself fully competent to render this dear cheek as faultless as its fellow; and then, most beloved, what will be my triumph when I shall have corrected what Nature left imperfect in her fairest work! Even Pygmalion, when his sculptured woman assumed life, felt not greater ecstasy than mine will be."

"It is resolved, then," said Georgiana, faintly smiling. "And, Aylmer, spare me not, though you should find the birthmark take refuge in my heart at last."

Her husband tenderly kissed her cheek — her right cheek, not that which bore the impress of the crimson hand.

The next day, Aylmer apprised his wife of a plan that he had formed whereby he might have opportunity for the intense thought and constant watchfulness which the proposed operation would require; while Georgiana, likewise, would enjoy the perfect repose essential to its success. They were to seclude themselves in the extensive apartments occupied by Aylmer as a laboratory, and where, during his toilsome youth, he had made discoveries in the elemental powers of Nature that had roused the admiration of all the learned societies in Europe. Seated calmly in this laboratory, the pale philosopher had investigated the secrets of the highest cloud region and of the profoundest mines; he had satisfied himself of the causes that kindled and kept alive the fires of the volcano; and had explained the mystery of fountains, and how it is that they gush forth, some so bright and pure, and others with such rich medicinal virtues, from the dark bosom of the earth. Here, too, at an earlier period, he had studied the wonders of the human frame, and attempted to fathom the very process by which Nature assimilates all her precious influences from earth and air, and from the spiritual world, to create and foster man, her masterpiece. The latter pursuit, however, Aylmer had long laid aside in unwilling recognition of the truth — against which all seekers sooner or later stumble — that our great creative Mother, while she amuses us with apparently working in the broadest sunshine, is yet severely careful to keep her own secrets, and, in spite of her pretended openness, shows us nothing but results. She permits us, indeed, to mar, but seldom to mend, and, like a jealous patentee, on no account to make. Now, however, Aylmer resumed these half-forgotten investigations; not, of course, with such hopes or wishes as first suggested them; but because they involved much physiological truth and lay in the path of his proposed scheme for the treatment of Georgiana.

As he led her over the threshold of the laboratory, Georgiana was cold and tremulous. Aylmer looked cheerfully into her face, with intent to reassure her, but was so startled with the intense glow of the birthmark upon the whiteness of her cheek that he could not restrain a strong, convulsive shudder. His wife fainted.

"Aminadab! Aminadab!" shouted Aylmer, stamping violently on the floor.

Forthwith there issued from an inner apartment a man of low stature, but bulky frame, with shaggy hair hanging about his visage, which was grimed with the vapors of the furnace. This personage had been Aylmer's underworker during his whole scientific career, and was admirably fitted for that office by his great mechanical readiness, and the skill with which, while incapable of comprehending a single principle, he executed all the details of his master's experiments. With his vast strength, his shaggy hair, his smoky aspect, and the indescribable earthiness that incrusted him, he seemed to represent man's physical nature; while Aylmer's slender figure, and pale, intellectual face, were no less apt a type of the spiritual element.

"Throw open the door of the boudoir, Aminadab," said Aylmer, "and burn a pastille."

"Yes, master," answered Aminadab, looking intently at the lifeless form of Georgiana; and then he muttered to himself, "If she were my wife, I'd never part with that birthmark."

When Georgiana recovered consciousness, she found herself breathing an atmosphere of penetrating fragrance, the gentle potency of which had recalled her from her deathlike faintness. The scene around her looked like enchantment. Aylmer had converted those smoky, dingy, somber rooms, where he had spent his brightest years in recondite pursuits, into a series of beautiful apartments not unfit to be the secluded abode of a lovely woman. The walls were hung with gorgeous curtains, which imparted the combination of grandeur and grace that no other species of adornment can achieve; and as they fell from the ceiling to the floor, their rich and ponderous folds, concealing all angles and straight lines, appeared to shut in the scene from infinite space. For aught Georgiana knew, it might be a pavilion among the clouds. And Aylmer, excluding the sunshine, which would have interfered with his chemical processes, had supplied its place with perfumed lamps, emitting flames of various hue, but all uniting in a soft, empurpled radiance. He now knelt by his wife's side, watching her earnestly, but without alarm; for he was confident in his science, and felt that he could draw a magic circle round her within which no evil might intrude.

"Where am I? Ah, I remember," said Georgiana, faintly; and she placed her hand over her cheek to hide the terrible mark from her husband's eyes.

"Fear not, dearest!" exclaimed he. "Do not shrink from me! Believe me, Georgiana, I even rejoice in this single imperfection, since it will be such a rapture to remove it."

"Oh, spare me!" sadly replied his wife. "Pray do not look at it again. I never can forget that convulsive shudder."

In order to soothe Georgiana, and, as it were, to release her mind from the burden of actual things, Aylmer now put in practice some of the light and playful secrets which science had taught him among its profounder lore. Airy figures, absolutely bodiless ideas, and forms of unsubstantial beauty came and danced before her, imprinting their momentary footsteps on beams of light. Though she had some indistinct idea of the method of these optical phenomena, still the illusion was almost perfect enough to warrant the belief that her husband possessed sway over the spiritual world. Then again, when she felt a wish to look forth from her seclusion, immediately, as if her thoughts were answered, the procession of external existence flitted across a screen. The scenery and the figures of actual life were perfectly represented, but with that bewitching yet indescribable difference which always makes a picture, an image, or a shadow so much more attractive than the original. When wearied of this, Aylmer bade her cast her eyes upon a vessel containing a quantity of earth. She did so, with little interest at first; but was soon startled to perceive the germ of a plant shooting upward from the soil. Then came the slender stalk; the leaves gradually unfolded themselves; and amid them was a perfect and lovely flower.

"It is magical!" cried Georgiana. "I dare not touch it."

"Nay, pluck it," answered Aylmer, "pluck it, and inhale its brief perfume while you may. The flower will wither in a few moments and leave nothing save its brown seed vessels; but thence may be perpetuated a race as ephemeral as itself."

But Georgiana had no sooner touched the flower than the whole plant suffered a blight, its leaves turning coal black as if by the agency of fire.

"There was too powerful a stimulus," said Aylmer, thoughtfully.

To make up for this abortive experiment, he proposed to take her portrait by a scientific process of his own invention. It was to be effected by rays of light striking upon a polished plate of metal. Georgiana assented; but, on looking at the results, was affrighted to find the features of the portrait blurred and indefinable; while the minute figure of a hand appeared where the cheek should have been. Aylmer snatched the metallic plate and threw it into a jar of corrosive acid.

Soon, however, he forgot these mortifying failures. In the intervals of study and chemical experiment, he came to her flushed and exhausted, but seemed invigorated by her presence, and spoke in glowing language of the resources of his art. He gave a history of the long dynasty of the alchemists, who spent so many ages in quest of the universal solvent by which the golden principle might be elicited from all things vile and base.

Aylmer appeared to believe that, by the plainest scientific logic, it was altogether within the limits of possibility to discover this long-sought medium; "but," he added, "a philosopher who should go deep enough to acquire the power would attain too lofty a wisdom to stoop to the exercise of it." Not less singular were his opinions in regard to the elixir vitae. He more than intimated that it was at his option to concoct a liquid that should prolong life for years, perhaps interminably; but that it would produce a discord in Nature which all the world, and chiefly the quaffer of the immortal nostrum, would find cause to curse.

"Aylmer, are you in earnest?" asked Georgiana, looking at him with amazement and fear. "It is terrible to possess such power, or even to dream of possessing it."

"Oh, do not tremble, my love," said her husband. "I would not wrong either you or myself by working such inharmonious effects upon our lives; but I would have you consider how trifling, in comparison, is the skill requisite to remove this little hand."

At the mention of the birthmark, Georgiana, as usual, shrank as if a red-hot iron had touched her cheek.

Again Aylmer applied himself to his labors. She could hear his voice in the distant furnace room, giving directions to Aminadab, whose harsh, uncouth, misshapen tones were audible in response, more like the grunt or growl of a brute than human speech. After hours of absence, Aylmer reappeared and proposed that she should now examine his cabinet of chemical products and natural treasures of the earth. Among the former he showed her a small vial, in which, he remarked, was contained a gentle yet most powerful fragrance, capable of impregnating all the breezes that blow across a kingdom. They were of inestimable value, the contents of that little vial; and, as he said so, he threw some of the perfume into the air and filled the room with piercing and invigorating delight.

"And what is this?" asked Georgiana, pointing to a small crystal globe containing a gold-colored liquid. "It is so beautiful to the eye that I could imagine it the elixir of life."

"In one sense it is," replied Aylmer, "or, rather, the elixir of immortality. It is the most precious poison that ever was concocted in this world. By its aid, I could apportion the lifetime of any mortal at whom you might point your finger.

The strength of the dose would determine whether he were to linger out years, or drop dead in the midst of a breath. No king on his guarded throne could keep his life if I, in my private station, should deem that the welfare of millions justified me in depriving him of it."

"Why do you keep such a terrific drug?" inquired Georgiana in horror.

"Do not mistrust me, dearest," said her husband, smiling. "Its virtuous potency is yet greater than its harmful one. But see! here is a powerful cosmetic. With a few drops of this in a vase of water, freckles may be washed away as easily as the hands are cleansed. A stronger infusion would take the blood out of the cheek, and leave the rosiest beauty a pale ghost."

"Is it with this lotion that you intend to bathe my cheek?" asked Georgiana, anxiously.

"Oh, no," hastily replied her husband, "this is merely superficial. Your case demands a remedy that shall go deeper."

In his interviews with Georgiana, Aylmer generally made minute inquiries as to her sensations and whether the confinement of the rooms and the temperature of the atmosphere agreed with her. These questions had such a particular drift that Georgiana began to conjecture that she was already subjected to certain physical influences, either breathed in with the fragrant air or taken with her food. She fancied likewise, but it might be altogether fancy, that there was a stirring up of her system — a strange, indefinite sensation creeping through her veins, and tingling, half painfully, half pleasurably, at her heart. Still, whenever she dared to look into the mirror, there she beheld herself pale as a white rose and with the crimson birthmark stamped upon her cheek. Not even Aylmer now hated it so much as she.

To dispel the tedium of the hours which her husband found it necessary to devote to the processes of combination and analysis, Georgiana turned over the volumes of his scientific library. In many dark old tomes she met with chapters full of romance and poetry. They were the works of the philosophers of the Middle Ages, such as Albertus Magnus, Cornelius Agrippa, Paracelsus, and the famous friar who created the prophetic Brazen Head. All these antique naturalists stood in advance of their centuries, yet were imbued with some of their credulity, and therefore were believed, and perhaps imagined themselves to have acquired from the investigation of Nature a power above Nature, and from physics a sway over the spiritual world. Hardly less curious and imaginative were the early volumes of the Transactions of the Royal Society, in which the members, knowing little of the limits of natural possibility, were continually recording wonders or proposing methods whereby wonders might be wrought.

But to Georgiana, the most engrossing volume was a large folio from her husband's own hand, in which he had recorded every experiment of his scientific career, its original aim, the methods adopted for its development, and its final success or failure, with the circumstances to which either event was attributable. The book, in truth, was both the history and emblem of his ardent, ambitious, imaginative, yet practical and laborious life. He handled physical details as if there were nothing beyond them; yet spiritualized them all, and redeemed himself from materialism by his strong and eager aspiration towards the infinite. In his grasp, the veriest clod of earth assumed a soul. Georgiana, as she read, reverenced Aylmer and loved him more profoundly than ever, but with a less entire dependence on his judgment than heretofore. Much as he had accomplished, she could not but observe that his most splendid successes were almost invariably failures, if compared with the ideal at which he aimed. His brightest diamonds were the merest pebbles, and felt to be so by himself, in comparison with the inestimable gems which lay hidden beyond his reach. The volume, rich with achievements that had won renown for its author, was yet as melancholy a record as ever mortal hand had penned. It was the sad confession and continual exemplification of the shortcomings of the composite man, the spirit burdened with clay and working in matter, and of the despair that assails the higher nature at finding itself so miserably thwarted by the earthly part. Perhaps every man of genius in whatever sphere might recognize the image of his own experience in Aylmer's journal.

So deeply did these reflections affect Georgiana that she laid her face upon the open volume and burst into tears. In this situation she was found by her husband.

"It is dangerous to read in a sorcerer's books," said he with a smile, though his countenance was uneasy and displeased. "Georgiana, there are pages in that volume which I can scarcely

glance over and keep my senses. Take heed lest it prove as
detrimental to you."

"It has made me worship you more than ever," said she.

"Ah, wait for this one success," rejoined he, "then worship
me if you will. I shall deem myself hardly unworthy of it. But
come, I have sought you for the luxury of your voice. Sing to
me, dearest."

So she poured out the liquid music of her voice to quench
the thirst of his spirit. He then took his leave with a boyish
exuberance of gaiety, assuring her that her seclusion would
endure but a little longer, and that the result was already
certain. Scarcely had he departed when Georgiana felt
irresistibly impelled to follow him. She had forgotten to inform
Aylmer of a symptom which for two or three hours past had
begun to excite her attention. It was a sensation in the fatal
birthmark, not painful, but which induced a restlessness
throughout her system. Hastening after her husband, she
intruded for the first time into the laboratory.

The first thing that struck her eye was the furnace, that hot
and feverish worker, with the intense glow of its fire, which by
the quantities of soot clustered above it seemed to have been
burning for ages. There was a distilling apparatus in full
operation. Around the room were retorts, tubes, cylinders,
crucibles, and other apparatus of chemical research. An
electrical machine stood ready for immediate use. The
atmosphere felt oppressively close, and was tainted with gaseous
odors which had been tormented forth by the processes of
science. The severe and homely simplicity of the apartment,
with its naked walls and brick pavement, looked strange,
accustomed as Georgiana had become to the fantastic elegance
of her boudoir. But what chiefly, indeed almost solely, drew her
attention was the aspect of Aylmer himself.

He was pale as death, anxious and absorbed, and hung over
the furnace as if it depended upon his utmost watchfulness
whether the liquid which it was distilling should be the draught
of immortal happiness or misery. How different from the
sanguine and joyous mien that he had assumed for Georgiana's
encouragement!

"Carefully now, Aminadab; carefully, thou human machine;
carefully, thou man of clay!" muttered Aylmer, more to
himself than his assistant. "Now, if there be a thought too much

or too little, it is all over."

"Ho! ho!" mumbled Aminadab. "Look, master! look!"

Aylmer raised his eyes hastily, and at first reddened, then grew paler than ever, on beholding Georgiana. He rushed towards her and seized her arm with a grip that left the print of his fingers upon it.

"Why do you come hither? Have you no trust in your husband?" cried he, impetuously. "Would you throw the blight of that fatal birthmark over my labors? It is not well done. Go, prying woman, go!"

"Nay, Aylmer," said Georgiana with the firmness of which she possessed no stinted endowment. "It is not you that have a right to complain. You mistrust your wife; you have concealed the anxiety with which you watch the development of this experiment. Think not so unworthily of me, my husband. Tell me all the risk we run, and fear not that I shall shrink; for my share in it is far less than your own."

"No, no, Georgiana!" said Aylmer, impatiently. "It must not be."

"I submit," replied she, calmly. "And, Aylmer, I shall quaff whatever draught you bring me; but it will be on the same principle that would induce me to take a dose of poison if offered by your hand."

"My noble wife," said Aylmer, deeply moved, "I knew not the height and depth of your nature until now. Nothing shall be concealed. Know, then, that this crimson hand, superficial as it seems, has clutched its grasp into your being with a strength of which I had no previous conception. I have already administered agents powerful enough to do aught except to change your entire physical system. Only one thing remains to be tried. If that fail us, we are ruined."

"Why did you hesitate to tell me this?" asked she.

"Because, Georgiana," said Aylmer, in a low voice, "there is danger."

"Danger? There is but one danger — that this horrible stigma shall be left upon my cheek!" cried Georgiana. "Remove it, remove it, whatever be the cost, or we shall both go mad!"

"Heaven knows your words are too true," said Aylmer, sadly. "And now, dearest, return to your boudoir. In a little while, all will be tested."

He conducted her back and took leave of her with a solemn

tenderness which spoke far more than his words how much was now at stake. After his departure, Georgiana became rapt in musings. She considered the character of Aylmer, and did it completer justice than at any previous moment. Her heart exulted, while it trembled, at his honorable love — so pure and lofty that it would accept nothing less than perfection nor miserably make itself contented with an earthlier nature than he had dreamed of. She felt how much more precious was such a sentiment than that meaner kind which would have borne with the imperfection for her sake, and have been guilty of treason to holy love by degrading its perfect idea to the level of the actual; and with her whole spirit, she prayed that, for a single moment, she might satisfy his highest and deepest conception. Longer than one moment she well knew it could not be; for his spirit was ever on the march, ever ascending, and each instant required something that was beyond the scope of the instant before.

The sound of her husband's footsteps aroused her. He bore a crystal goblet containing a liquor colorless as water, but bright enough to be the draught of immortality. Aylmer was pale; but it seemed rather the consequence of a highly wrought state of mind and tension of spirit than of fear or doubt.

"The concoction of the draught has been perfect," said he, in answer to Georgiana's look. "Unless all my science have deceived me, it cannot fail."

"Save on your account, my dearest Aylmer," observed his wife, "I might wish to put off this birthmark of mortality by relinquishing mortality itself in preference to any other mode. Life is but a sad possession to those who have attained precisely the degree of moral advancement at which I stand. Were I weaker and blinder, it might be happiness. Were I stronger, it might be endured hopefully. But, being what I find myself, methinks I am of all mortals the most fit to die."

"You are fit for heaven without tasting death!" replied her husband. "But why do we speak of dying? The draught cannot fail. Behold its effect upon this plant."

On the window seat there stood a geranium diseased with yellow blotches, which had overspread all its leaves. Aylmer poured a small quantity of the liquid upon the soil in which it grew. In a little time, when the roots of the plant had taken up the moisture, the unsightly blotches began to be extinguished in a living verdure.

"There needed no proof," said Georgiana, quietly. "Give me the goblet. I joyfully stake all upon your word."

"Drink, then, thou lofty creature!" exclaimed Aylmer, with fervid admiration. "There is no taint of imperfection on thy spirit. Thy sensible frame, too, shall soon be all perfect."

She quaffed the liquid and returned the goblet to his hand.

"It is grateful," said she, with a placid smile. "Methinks it is like water from a heavenly fountain; for it contains I know not what of unobtrusive fragrance and deliciousness. It allays a feverish thirst that had parched me for many days. Now, dearest, let me sleep. My earthly senses are closing over my spirit like the leaves around the heart of a rose at sunset."

She spoke the last words with a gentle reluctance, as if it required almost more energy than she could command to pronounce the faint and lingering syllables. Scarcely had they loitered through her lips ere she was lost in slumber. Aylmer sat by her side, watching her aspect with the emotions proper to a man the whole value of whose existence was involved in the process now to be tested. Mingled with this mood, however, was the philosophic investigation characteristic of the man of science. Not the minutest symptom escaped him. A heightened flush of the cheek, a slight irregularity of breath, a quiver of the eyelid, a hardly perceptible tremor through the frame — such were the details which, as the moments passed, he wrote down in his folio volume. Intense thought had set its stamp upon every previous page of that volume, but the thoughts of years were all concentrated upon the last.

While thus employed, he failed not to gaze often at the fatal hand, and not without a shudder. Yet once, by a strange and unaccountable impulse, he pressed it with his lips. His spirit recoiled, however, in the very act; and Georgiana, out of the midst of her deep sleep, moved uneasily and murmured as if in remonstrance. Again Aylmer resumed his watch. Nor was it without avail. The crimson hand, which at first had been strongly visible upon the marble paleness of Georgiana's cheek, now grew more faintly outlined. She remained not less pale than ever; but the birthmark, with every breath that came and went, lost somewhat of its former distinctness. Its presence had been awful; its departure was more awful still. Watch the stain of the rainbow fading out of the sky, and you will know how that mysterious symbol passed away.

"By Heaven! it is well-nigh gone!" said Aylmer to himself, in almost irrepressible ecstasy. "I can scarcely trace it now. Success! success! And now it is like the faintest rose color. The lightest flush of blood across her cheek would overcome it. But she is so pale!"

He drew aside the window curtain and suffered the light of natural day to fall into the room and rest upon her cheek. At the same time, he heard a gross, hoarse chuckle, which he had long known as his servant Aminadab's expression of delight.

"Ah, clod! Ah, earthly mass!" cried Aylmer, laughing in a sort of frenzy, "you have served me well! Matter and spirit — earth and heaven — have both done their part in this! Laugh, thing of the senses! You have earned the right to laugh."

These exclamations broke Georgiana's sleep. She slowly unclosed her eyes and gazed into the mirror which her husband had arranged for that purpose. A faint smile flitted over her lips when she recognized how barely perceptible was now that crimson hand which had once blazed forth with such disastrous brilliancy as to scare away all their happiness. But then her eyes sought Aylmer's face with a trouble and anxiety that he could by no means account for.

"My poor Aylmer!" murmured she.

"Poor? Nay, richest, happiest, most favored!" exclaimed he. "My peerless bride, it is successful! You are perfect!"

"My poor Aylmer," she repeated, with a more than human tenderness, "you have aimed loftily; you have done nobly. Do not repent that with so high and pure a feeling, you have rejected the best the earth could offer. Aylmer, dearest Aylmer, I am dying!"

Alas! it was too true! The fatal hand had grappled with the mystery of life, and was the bond by which an angelic spirit kept itself in union with a mortal frame. As the last crimson tint of the birthmark — that sole token of human imperfection — faded from her cheek, the parting breath of the now perfect woman passed into the atmosphere, and her soul, lingering a moment near her husband, took its heavenward flight. Then a hoarse, chuckling laugh was heard again! Thus ever does the gross fatality of earth exult in its invariable triumph over the immortal essence which, in this dim sphere of half development, demands the completeness of a higher state. Yet, had Aylmer reached a profounder wisdom, he need not thus have flung away the happiness which would have woven his mortal life of the selfsame texture with the celestial. The momentary circumstance was too strong for him; he failed to look beyond the shadowy scope of time, and, living once for all in eternity, to find the perfect future in the present.

ALIBRATIONS

THE WELL AT THE WORLD'S
END by William Morris. 2 vols.
Ballantine 01982 and 02015, New
York, 1970. Paper, 320 and 242 pp.
$.95 each.

SOME books survive just for their
usefulness, and others because they are
representative of their times, and there are a few, a very few, that outlast
the years from sheer beauty of composition. THE WELL AT THE
WORLD'S END is such a book: its calm brilliance, its quiet, gentle people,
its almost-Medieval world, one step the other side of reality, are enough to
take one's breath away. In some respects it is neither an easy book to read
nor to judge: originally published in 1896, it is long, one of the longest
heroic fantasies ever penned; it is written in a purposely archaic tongue,
created and patterned after Medieval English; its pace and rhythm are
considerably slower than most modern readers are accustomed to; and its
plot and resolution, which seem on the surface perhaps overly simplified
or romanticized, are in reality exceedingly complex and interwoven. Yet
for all these "defects," if they are defects, THE WELL remains one of the
finest examples of its *genre*, a true classic of imaginative literature.

Superficially, it is a quest story, telling of one Ralph, son to the Kinglet
of Upmeads, and how he came to the Well at the World's End, and what
became thereof; but it would not be stretching matters to say that the
book celebrates the journey of a boy into the world, and his discovery of
himself and what it means to be a man — a journey that every man must
take. As such, the work has universal application and meaning, particularly
in a time as seething and unsettling as our own. It may be difficult for us
to visualize the Victorian period as one of upheaval, but to Morris it
certainly was. He deeply resented the materialism of his age, the
mass-merchandizing which he believed dehumanized the ordinary worker
into just another cog in the industrial machine. In the face of continual
change, Morris found only one thing constant: the beauty of a simple and
uncomplicated way of life, a beauty he believed was incarnated in the
Medieval period, a beauty he embraced with his entire soul. In a way he
never grew up.

This is not a book to swallow down in gulps. Sip at it slowly, gradually — let it softly overcome your mind. You will find both sex and violence in it — Morris was far from being a prude — but you will also uncover something rarely seen in today's literature: a deep sense of peace and surety in man and the world. And wonder, that something so filled with beauty could exist in words. There are those who say it is impossible to love a book. However that may be, if it *is* possible, here is one well worth the devotion.

RR

BEWARE THE BEASTS, Edited by Vic Ghidalia and Roger Elwood. Macfadden 00343, New York, 1970. Paper, 160 pp. $.75.
Ignore the bad blurbs and the mediocre cover — this is a fine anthology of horror tales based around the theme of a beast or creature as the central point of each story. There are natural beasts in unnatural contexts, such as the cats in Lovecraft's "The Cats of Ulthar," Bram Stoker's chilling "The Squaw," and Greye La Spina's "The Tortoise-Shell Cat," from an early WEIRD TALES. And there are what-is-it-type beasts, too, such as in H. G. Wells' "In the Avu Observatory," and Algernon Blackwood's classic, "The Wendigo." Other chillers by August Derleth, Edgar Allan Poe, Rudyard Kipling, Edward Lucas White, and Fritz Leiber round out a collection that is heartily recommended to all shudder-seekers.

BEFORE ADAM by Jack London. Ace 05330, New York, 1970. Paper, 228 pp. $.75.
Last issue I mentioned the Bantam edition of this fine prehistoric adventure classic; now Ace has come out with an edition that you'll probably want, even if you bought the other one. Why? Smart merchandising: the Ace edition has reproduced the original Charles Livingston Bull illustrations, and given us an excellent cover by Jerome Podwil, probably his best to date. Most dealers place both editions in the literature section, along with London's other works, so don't look for them in the SF section.

THE UNTAMED by Max Brand. Pocket Books 55071, New York, 1970. Paper, 186 pp. $.60.
"A western? You're kidding!" Yes, a western — one of the best ever written — and I'm not kidding. This book is also one of the finest and most subtle fantasy novels ever written (see "Excavations," this issue). It is the first of a trilogy about Whistling Dan Barry, a strange, wild man with a more-than-human rapport with his great horse Satan and his savage wolf companion, Black Bart, and possessed of strength, agility and speed beyond belief. Even if you don't care for westerns (as I don't), try this one, and see if you aren't caught up in the story of "Pan of the Desert."

DM

MAN—SIZE IN MARBLE

by E. Nesbit

Illustrated by Bill Hughes

E(DITH) NESBIT (1858 - 1924) was born in London into a large family of brothers and sisters, and soon became an incorrigible and outspoken tomboy, involved in one escapade after another. It was these childhood experiences upon which she later drew that helped to make her one of the most popular children's authors of the early twentieth century. Edith's father died when she was only three, and she subsequently attended many different schools in England, France and Germany. The family returned to England, and Edith, now a vivacious and beautiful young girl, became passionately interested in literature and political reform. Her first poem, "The Dawn," was published when she was only seventeen, and in 1880 she married Hubert Bland, a journalist, and became with him a pioneer member of the Socialist Fabian Society, which also included among its membership Bernard Shaw and H. G. Wells. Edith's husband apparently belied his name, alternating between bouts of flagrant infidelity and serious illness. In order to earn a living, Edith was forced to turn to

writing, producing love stories, novels, Christmas card verse — anything
that would sell. Finally, however, she hit upon the kind of story that was
natural to her and that she truly enjoyed writing: stories for and about
children. With the publication in book form of THE TREASURE
SEEKERS in 1899 by "E. Nesbit," she embarked upon a career which
produced some of the most beloved children's literature of all time. Edith
soon began to introduce an element of magic and fantasy into her stories,
which made them even more popular. Such books as FIVE CHILDREN
AND IT (1902), THE PHOENIX AND THE CARPET (1904), THE
STORY OF THE AMULET (1906), and THE ENCHANTED CASTLE
(1907) can be read and appreciated by adults as well as children as lively,
witty fantasies that never condescend or preach. Most of them are still in
print today. However, all but lost to us are several volumes of horror
stories which Edith produced early in her writing career, when times were
hard and her life an emotional turmoil. We see the dark side of this
charming woman expressed most vividly in the following story from her
collection GRIM TALES, published in 1893.

ALTHOUGH every word of this story is as true as despair, I do
not expect people to believe it. Nowadays a 'rational
explanation' is required before belief is possible. Let me, then,
at once offer the 'rational explanation' which finds most favour
among those who have heard the tale of my life's tragedy. It is
held that we were 'under a delusion,' Laura and I, on that 31st
of October; and that this supposition places the whole matter
on a satisfactory and believable basis. The reader can judge,
when he, too, has heard my story, how far this is an
'explanation,' and in what sense it is 'rational.' There were three
who took part in this: Laura and I and another man. The other
man still lives, and can speak to the truth of the least credible
part of my story.

I never in my life knew what it was to have as much money as I
required to supply the most ordinary needs — good colours,
books, and cab-fares — and when we were married we knew
quite well that we should only be able to live at all by 'strict
punctuality and attention to business.' I used to paint in those
days, and Laura used to write, and we felt sure we could keep
the pot at least simmering. Living in town was out of the
question, so we went to look for a cottage in the country,
which should be at once sanitary and picturesque. So rarely do
these two qualities meet in one cottage that our search was for

some time quite fruitless. But when we got away from friends and house-agents, on our honeymoon, our wits grew clear again, and we knew a pretty cottage when at last we saw one.

It was at Brenzett — a little village set on a hill over against the southern marshes. We had gone there, from the seaside village where we were staying, to see the church, and two fields from the church we found this cottage. It stood quite by itself, about two miles from the village. It was a long, low building, with rooms sticking out in unexpected places. There was a bit of stone-work — ivy-covered and moss-grown, just two old rooms, all that was left of a big house that had once stood there — and round this stone-work the house had grown up. Stripped of its roses and jasmine it would have been hideous. As it stood it was charming, and after a brief examination we took it. It was absurdly cheap. There was a jolly old-fashioned garden, with grass paths, and no end of hollyhocks and sunflowers, and big lilies. From the window you could see the marsh-pastures, and beyond them the blue, thin line of the sea.

We got a tall old peasant woman to do for us. Her face and figure were good, though her cooking was of the homeliest; but she understood all about gardening, and told us all the old names of the coppices and cornfields, and the stories of the smugglers and highwaymen, and, better still, of the 'things that walked,' and of the 'sights' which met one in lonely glens of a starlight night. We soon came to leave all the domestic business to Mrs. Dorman, and to use her legends in little magazine stories which brought in the jingling guinea.

We had three months of married happiness, and did not have a single quarrel. One October evening I had been down to smoke a pipe with the doctor — our only neighbour — a pleasant young Irishman. Laura had stayed at home to finish a comic sketch. I left her laughing over her own jokes, and came in to find her a crumpled heap of pale muslin, weeping on the window seat.

'Good heavens, my darling, what's the matter?' I cried, taking her in my arms. 'What is the matter? Do speak.'

'It's Mrs. Dorman,' she sobbed.

'What has she done?' I inquired, immensely relieved.

'She says she must go before the end of the month, and she says her niece is ill; she's gone down to see her now, but I don't believe that's the reason, because her niece is always ill. I believe someone has been setting her against us. Her manner was so queer —'

'Never mind, Pussy,' I said; 'whatever you do, don't cry, or I shall have to cry too to keep you in countenance, and then you'll never respect your man again.'

'But you see,' she went on, 'it is really serious, because these village people are so sheepy, and if one won't do a thing you may be quite sure none of the others will. And I shall have to cook the dinners and wash up the hateful greasy plates; and you'll have to carry cans of water about and clean the boots and knives — and we shall never have any time for work or earn any money or anything.'

I represented to her that even if we had to perform these duties the day would still present some margin or other toils and recreations. But she refused to see the matter in any but the greyest light.

'I'll speak to Mrs. Dorman when she comes back, and see if I can't come to terms with her,' I said. 'Perhaps she wants a rise. It will be all right. Let's walk up to the church.'

The church was a large and lonely one, and we loved to go there, especially upon bright nights. The path skirted a wood, cut through it once, and ran along the crest of the hill through two meadows, and round the churchyard wall, over which the old yews loomed in black masses of shadow.

This path, which was partly paved, was called 'the bier-walk,' for it had long been the way by which the corpses had been carried to burial. The churchyard was richly treed, and was shaded by great elms which stood just outside and stretched their majestic arms in benediction over the happy dead. A large, low porch let one into the building by a Norman doorway and a heavy oak door studded with iron. Inside, the arches rose into darkness, and between them the reticulated windows, which stood out white in the moonlight. In the chancel, the windows were of rich glass, which showed in faint light their noble colouring, and made the black oak of the choir pews hardly more solid than the shadows. But on each side of the altar lay a grey marble figure of a knight in full plate armour lying upon a low slab, with hands held up in everlasting prayer, and these figures, oddly enough, were always to be seen if there was any glimmer of light in the church. Their names were lost, but the peasants told of them that they had been fierce and wicked

men, marauders by land and sea, who had been the scourge of
their time, and had been guilty of deeds so foul that the house
they had lived in — the big house, by the way, that had stood
on the site of our cottage — had been stricken by lightning and
the vengeance of Heaven. But for all that, the gold of their heirs
had bought them a place in the church. Looking at the bad,
hard faces reproduced in the marble, this story was easily
believed.

The church looked at its best and weirdest on that night, for
the shadows of the yew trees fell through the windows upon the
floor of the nave and touched the pillars with tattered shade.
We sat down together without speaking, and watched the
solemn beauty of the old church with some of that awe which
inspired its early builders. We walked to the chancel and looked
at the sleeping warriors. Then we rested some time on the stone
seat in the porch, looking out over the stretch of quiet moonlit
meadows, feeling in every fibre of our being the peace of the
night and of our happy love; and came away at last with a sense
that even scrubbing and black-leading were but small troubles at
their worst.

Mrs. Dorman had come back from the village, and I at once
invited her to a *tete-a-tete.*

'Now, Mrs. Dorman,' I said, when I had got her into my
painting room, 'what's all this about your not staying with us?'

'I should be glad to get away, sir, before the end of the
month,' she answered, with her usual placid dignity.

'Have you any fault to find, Mrs. Dorman?'

'None at all, sir: you and your lady have always been most
kind, I'm sure —'

'Well, what is it? Are your wages not high enough?'

'No, sir, I gets quite enough.'

'Then why not stay?'

'I'd rather not' — with some hesitation — 'my niece is ill.'

'But your niece has been ill ever since we came. Can't you
stay for another month?'

'No, sir, I'm bound to go by Thursday.'

And this was Monday!

'Well, I must say, I think you might have let us know before.
There's no time now to get anyone else, and your mistress is not
fit to do heavy housework. Can't you stay till next week?'

'I might be able to come back next week.'

'But why must you go this week?' I persisted. 'Come out with it.'

Mrs. Dorman drew the little shawl, which she always wore, tightly across her bosom, as though she were cold. Then she said, with a sort of effort:

'They say, sir, as this was a big house in Catholic times, and there was a many deeds done here.'

The nature of the 'deeds' might be vaguely inferred from the inflection of Mrs. Dorman's voice — which was enough to make one's blood run cold. I was glad that Laura was not in the room. She was always nervous, as highly-strung natures are, and I felt that these tales about our house, told by this old peasant woman, with her impressive manner and contagious credulity, might have made our home less dear to my wife.

'Tell me all about it, Mrs. Dorman,' I said; 'you needn't mind about telling me. I'm not like the young people who make fun of such things.'

Which was partly true.

'Well, sir' — she sank her voice — 'you may have seen in the church, beside the altar, two shapes.'

'You mean the effigies of the knights in armour,' I said cheerfully.

'I mean them two bodies, drawed out man-size in marble,' she returned, and I had to admit that her description was a thousand times more graphic than mine, to say nothing of a certain weird force and uncanniness about the phrase 'drawed out man-size in marble.'

'They do say, as on All Saints' Eve them two bodies sits up on their slabs, and gets off of them, and then walks down the aisle, *in their marble*' — (another good phrase, Mrs. Dorman) — 'and as the church clock strikes eleven they walks out of the church door, and over the graves, and along the bier-walk, and if it's a wet night there's the marks of their feet in the morning.'

'And where do they go?' I asked, rather fascinated.

'They comes back here to their home, sir, and if anyone meets them —'

'Well, what then?' I asked.

But no — not another word could I get from her, save that her niece was ill and she must go.

'Whatever you do, sir, lock the door early on All Saints' Eve, and make the cross-sign over the doorstep and on the windows.'

'But has anyone ever seen these things?' I persisted. 'Who was here last year?'

'No one, sir; the lady as owned the house only stayed here in summer, and she always went to London a full month afore *the* night. And I'm sorry to inconvenience you and your lady, but my niece is ill and I must go Thursday.'

I could have shaken her for her absurd reiteration of that obvious fiction, after she had told me her real reasons.

I did not tell Laura the legend of the shapes that 'walked in their marble,' partly because a legend concerning our house might perhaps trouble my wife, and partly, I think, from some more occult reason. This was not quite the same to me as any other story, and I did not want to talk about it till the day was over. I had very soon ceased to think of the legend, however. I was painting a portrait of Laura, against the lattice window, and I could not think of much else. I had got a splendid background of yellow and grey sunset, and was working away with enthusiasm at her face. On Thursday Mrs. Dorman went. She relented, at parting, so far as to say:

'Don't you put yourself about too much, ma'am, and if there's any little thing I can do next week I'm sure I shan't mind.'

Thursday passed off pretty well. Friday came. It is about what happened on that Friday that this is written.

I got up early, I remember, and lighted the kitchen fire, and had just achieved a smoky success when my little wife came running down as sunny and sweet as the clear October morning itself. We prepared breakfast together, and found it very good fun. The housework was soon done, and when brushes and brooms and pails were quiet again the house was still indeed. It is wonderful what a difference one makes in a house. We really missed Mrs. Dorman, quite apart from considerations concerning pots and pans. We spent the day in dusting our books and putting them straight, and dined on cold steak and coffee. Laura was, if possible, brighter and gayer and sweeter than usual, and I began to think that a little domestic toil was really good for her. We had never been so merry since we were married, and the walk we had that afternoon was, I think, the happiest time of all my life. When we had watched the deep scarlet clouds slowly pale into leaden grey against a pale green sky and saw the white mists curl up along the hedgerows in the distant marsh we came back to the house hand in hand.

'You are sad, my darling,' I said, half-jestingly, as we sat down together in our little parlour. I expected a disclaimer, for my own silence had been the silence of complete happiness. To my surprise she said:

'Yes, I think I am sad, or, rather, I am uneasy. I don't think I'm very well. I have shivered three or four times since we came in; and it is not cold, is it?'

'No,' I said, and hoped it was not a chill caught from the treacherous mists that roll up from the marshes in the dying night. No — she said, she did not think so. Then, after a silence, she spoke suddenly:

'Do you ever have presentiments of evil?'

'No,' I said, smiling, 'and I shouldn't believe in them if I had.'

'I do,' she went on, 'the night my father died I knew it, though he was right away in the North of Scotland.' I did not answer in words.

She sat looking at the fire for some time in silence, gently stroking my hand. At last she sprang up, came behind me, and, drawing my head back, kissed me.

'There, it's over now,' she said. 'What a baby I am! Come, light the candles, and we'll have some of these new Rubinstein duets.'

And we spent a happy hour or two at the piano.

At about half past ten I began to long for the good-night pipe, but Laura looked so white that I felt it would be brutal of me to fill our sitting-room with the fumes of strong cavendish.

'I'll take my pipe outside,' I said.

'Let me come, too.'

'No, sweetheart, not tonight; you're much too tired. I shan't be long. Get to bed, or I shall have an invalid to nurse tomorrow as well as the boots to clean.'

I kissed her and was turning to go when she flung her arms round my neck and held me as if she would never let me go again. I stroked her hair.

'Come, Pussy, you're over-tired. The housework has been too much for you.'

She loosened her clasp a little and drew a deep breath.

'No. We've been very happy today, Jack, haven't we? Don't stay out too long.'

'I won't, my dearie.'

I strolled out of the front door, leaving it unlatched. What a
night it was! The jagged masses of heavy dark cloud were rolling
at intervals from horizon to horizon, and thin white wreaths
covered the stars. Through all the rush of the cloud river the
moon swam, breasting the waves and disappearing again in the
darkness.

I walked up and down, drinking in the beauty of the quiet
earth and the changing sky. The night was absolutely silent.
Nothing seemed to be abroad. There was no scurrying of
rabbits, or twitter of the half-asleep birds. And though the
clouds went sailing across the sky, the wind that drove them
never came low enough to rustle the dead leaves in the
woodland paths. Across the meadows I could see the church
tower standing out black and grey against the sky. I walked
there thinking over our three months of happiness.

I heard a bell-beat from the church. Eleven already! I turned
to go in, but the night held me. I could not go back into our
warm rooms yet. I would go up to the church.

I looked in at the low window as I went by. Laura was half
lying on her chair in front of the fire. I could not see her face,
only her little head showed dark against the pale blue wall. She
was quite still. Asleep, no doubt.

I walked slowly along the edge of the wood. A sound broke
the stillness of the night, it was a rustling in the wood. I stopped
and listened. The sound stopped too. I went on, and now
distinctly heard another step than mine answer mine like an
echo. It was a poacher or a wood-stealer, most likely, for these
were not unknown in our Arcadian neighbourhood. But
whoever it was, he was a fool not to step more lightly. I turned
into the wood and now the footstep seemed to come from the
path I had just left. It must be an echo, I thought. The wood
looked perfect in the moonlight. The large dying ferns and the
brushwood showed where through thinning foliage the pale
light came down. The tree trunks stood up like Gothic columns
all around me. They reminded me of the church, and I turned
into the bier-walk, and passed through the corpse-gate between
the graves to the low porch.

I paused for a moment on the stone seat where Laura and I
had watched the fading landscape. Then I noticed that the door
of the church was open, and I blamed myself for having left it
unlatched the other night. We were the only people who ever

cared to come to the church except on Sundays, and I was
vexed to think that through our carelessness the damp autumn
airs had had a chance of getting in and injuring the old fabric. I
went in. It will seem strange, perhaps, that I should have gone
half way up the aisle before I remembered — with a sudden
chill, followed by as sudden a rush of self-contempt — that this
was the very day and hour when, according to tradition, the
'shapes drawed out man-size in marble' began to walk.

Having thus remembered the legend, and remembered it with
a shiver, of which I was ashamed, I could not do otherwise than
walk up towards the altar, just to look at the figures — as I said
to myself; really what I wanted was to assure myself, first, that
I did not believe the legend, and secondly, that it was not true. I
was rather glad that I had come. I thought now I could tell Mrs.
Dorman how vain her fancies were, and how peacefully the
marble figures slept on through the ghastly hour. With my
hands in my pockets I passed up the aisle. In the grey dim light
the eastern end of the church looked larger than usual, and the
arches above the two tombs looked larger too. The moon came
out and showed me the reason. I stopped short, my heart gave a
leap that nearly choked me, and then sank sickeningly.

The 'bodies drawed out man-size' *were gone!* and their
marble slabs lay wide and bare in the vague moonlight that
slanted through the east window.

Were they really gone, or was I mad? Clenching my nerves, I
stooped and passed my hand over the smooth slabs and felt
their flat unbroken surface. Had someone taken the things
away? Was it some vile practical joke? I would make sure,
anyway. In an instant I had made a torch of newspaper, which
happened to be in my pocket, and, lighting it, held it high above
my head. Its yellow glare illumined the dark arches and those
slabs. The figures *were* gone. And I was alone in the church; or
was I alone?

And then a horror seized me, a horror indefinable and
indescribable — an overwhelming certainty of supreme and
accomplished calamity. I flung down the torch and tore along
the aisle and out through the porch, biting my lips as I ran to
keep myself from shrieking aloud. Oh, was I mad — or what was
this that possessed me? I leaped the churchyard wall and took
the straight cut across the fields, led by the light from our
windows. Just as I got over the first stile a dark figure seemed to

spring out of the ground. Mad still with that certainty of misfortune, I made for the thing that stood in my path, shouting, 'Get out of the way, can't you!'

But my push met with a more vigorous resistance than I had expected. My arms were caught just above the elbow and held as in a vice, and the raw-boned Irish doctor actually shook me.

'Let me go, you fool,' I gasped. 'The marble figures have gone from the church; I tell you they've gone.'

He broke into a ringing laugh. 'I'll have to give you a draught tomorrow, I see. Ye've bin smoking too much and listening to old wives' tales.'

'I tell you, I've seen the bare slabs.'

'Well, come back with me. I'm going up to old Palmer's — his daughter's ill; we'll look in at the church and let me see the bare - slabs.'

'You go, if you like,' I said, a little less frantic for his laughter; 'I'm going home to my wife.'

'Rubbish, man,' said he; 'd'ye think I'll permit of that? Are ye to go saying all yer life that ye've seen solid marble endowed with vitality, and me to go all me life saying ye were a coward? No, sir — ye shan't do ut.'

The night air — a human voice — and I think also the physical contact with this six feet of solid common sense, brought me back to my ordinary self, and the word 'coward' was a mental shower-bath.

'Come on, then,' I said sullenly; 'perhaps you're right.'

He still held my arm tightly. We got over the stile and back to the church. All was still as death. The place smelt very damp and earthly. We walked up the aisle. I am not ashamed to confess that I shut my eyes: I knew the figures would not be there. I heard Kelly strike a match.

'Here they are, ye see, right enough; ye've been dreaming or drinking, asking yer pardon for the imputation.'

I opened my eyes. By Kelly's expiring vesta I saw two shapes lying 'in their marble' on their slabs. I drew a deep breath.

'I'm awfully indebted to you,' I said. 'It must have been some trick of light, or I have been working rather hard, perhaps that's it. I was quite convinced they were gone.'

'I'm aware of that,' he answered rather grimly; 'ye'll have to be careful of that brain of yours, my friend, I assure ye.'

He was leaning over and looking at the right-hand figure,

whose stony face was the most villainous and deadly in expression.

'By Jove,' he said, 'something has been afoot here — this hand is broken.'

And so it was. I was certain that it had been perfect the last time Laura and I had been there.

'Perhaps someone has *tried* to remove them,' said the young doctor.

'Come along,' I said, 'or my wife will be getting anxious. You'll come in and have a drop of whisky and drink confusion to ghosts and better sense to me.'

'I ought to go up to Palmer's, but it's so late now I'd best leave it till the morning,' he replied.

I think he fancied I needed him more than did Palmer's girl, so, discussing how such an illusion could have been possible, and deducing from this experience large generalities concerning ghostly apparitions, we walked up to our cottage. We saw, as we walked up the garden path, that bright light streamed out of the front door, and presently saw that the parlour door was open, too. Had she gone out?

'Come in,' I said, and Dr. Kelly followed me into the parlour. It was all ablaze with candles, not only the wax ones, but at least a dozen guttering, glaring tallow dips, stuck in vases and ornaments in unlikely places. Light, I knew, was Laura's remedy for nervousness. Poor child! Why had I left her? Brute that I was.

We glanced round the room, and at first we did not see her. The window was open, and the draught set all the candles flaring one way. Her chair was empty and her handkerchief and book lay on the floor. I turned to the window. There, in the recess of the window, I saw her. Oh, my child, my love, had she gone to that window to watch for me? And what had come into the room behind her? To what had she turned with that look of frantic fear and horror? Oh, my little one, had she thought that it was I whose step she heard, and turned to meet — what?

She had fallen back across a table in the window, and her body lay half on it and half on the window-seat, and her head hung down over the table, the brown hair loosened and fallen to the carpet. Her lips were drawn back, and her eyes wide, wide open. They saw nothing now. What had they seen last?

The doctor moved towards her, but I pushed him aside and

sprang to her; caught her in my arms and cried:

'It's all right, Laura! I've got you safe, wifie.'

She fell into my arms in a heap. I clasped her and kissed her, and called her by pet names, but I think I knew all the time that she was dead. Her hands were tightly clenched. In one of them she held something fast. When I was quite sure that she was dead, and that nothing mattered at all any more, I let him open her hand to see what she held.

It was a grey marble finger.

The ship in company with a vast volume of water sprang
into the air to a great height.

THE
Goddess of Atvatabar

BY

WILLIAM R. BRADSHAW

(PART III)

SYNOPSIS

The Arctic exploration ship *Polar King*, owned and commanded by Lexington White, and carrying an able company of officers and scientists, has attempted to reach the North Pole, but instead has sailed through a strange polar opening into an incredible interior world. They make contact with the inhabitants of Atvatabar, a continent of the interior world, and are accepted as peaceful visitors. They are then taken to Kioram, the principal port of Atvatabar, where they are welcomed enthusiastically by the governor and the populace. After a sumptuous feast, White and his men journey to Calnogar, the capital of Atvatabar, on the "Sacred Locomotive," a fantastic monorail car powered by a force called "magnicity." Upon arriving at the king's palace, they are warmly welcomed by the monarch and his queen, and are given a tour of the wonders of Atvatabar, during which they are awed by the magnificent art and architecture, advanced scientific devices, and strange but beautiful religious concepts of the inner world. Finally, they are introduced to the beautiful Lyone, living symbol of religious worship, the Goddess of Atvatabar. Lyone is as gracious as she is beautiful, and curious to learn about the outside world. Lexington White gladly assumes the role of tutor, and to his mixed consternation and delight, discovers himself falling hopelessly in love with the goddess. Lyone shows White the strange plant-animals that grow in her garden, then offers to take him and his officers to the city of Egyplosis with her, to witness an important religious ceremony. Aboard her aerial yacht, they barely escape destruction by a cyclone, but finally arrive safely at the Grand Temple of Harikar. There they witness the installation of a twin soul, a ceremony in which two young lovers are united in a state of perfect spiritual love, a Nirvana on earth. White is impressed, but argues with the goddess against platonic, spiritual love at the expense of natural, physical love. Before she can reply, they are interrupted as a pair of young lovers are brought before her for judgement, bearing a newborn baby as proof of their crime: daring to love each other as man and wife. The stern high priest orders them imprisoned separately for life, but the gentle goddess pleads for mercy.

CHAPTER XXXIII.

THE DOCTOR'S OPINION OF EGYPLOSIS.

MY experiences in Egyplosis were teaching me that even the most perfect human organizations contain the elements of decay and death. The human soul at variance with its own physical condition was hardly the best ideal of a god. Here was happiness piled upon happiness, yet the recipients thereof were not happy. Disappointments and suffering are natural to man because life is supported on difficulty, and a long-continued happiness is the sure forerunner of disaster. The reaction of misery lies somewhere concealed from the eye of happiness, and if it does not at once show itself, it will later on. Even in well-guarded happiness, if one single pleasure be omitted, we experience more regret at its absence than pleasure over the bounties we enjoy. Hence, a large proportion of twin-souls were not wholly in love with their life in the temple of souls, however enamored they were of each other. Almost absolute freedom of action, freedom from care, physical and mental exercises, soul development, the practice of magic, the most alluring investigation of mental and spiritual themes, the study and practice of art in all its forms, and the investigation of inventive mechanism; a palace to live in, with vast galleries of paintings and sculptures, salons for music, and schools of science, libraries filled with the rarest works of history, literature and poetry, and, most precious of all, the daily dalliance with counterpart souls, could not make these people happy. The one thing denied, which any reasonable man would say was simply the price paid for all this glory, was considered the greatest of all misfortunes. The imagination has a strange habit of passing lightly over happiness possessed and settling down upon a little thing beyond reach and exaggerating it to the utmost.

The imprisonment of Ardsolus and Merga created a profound sensation among the ten thousand inmates of the palace. Sentiment was divided so much that two political parties were formed — those who believed the erring lovers had met a just fate, and those who thought the system at fault in providing no means of immediate escape, when to reside in the palace became imprisonment and a living death to certain souls. The latter party was composed of the more youthful section of the priesthood, who sympathized with the unfortunate lovers. These latter would have got up a demonstration in their favor did not the stern rules of Egyplosis suppress any such outbursts of popular feeling.

On the day following the imprisonment of the erring twin-soul, the question was being discussed in the apartments occupied by the officers of the *Polar King* and myself. We had been lodged in a noble building not far from the palace of the goddess, while the sailors were quartered in the fortress of Egypolsis, in company with the wayleals of the palace itself.

"Your opinion of Egyplosis has possibly undergone a change since the day of our reception," said the doctor.

"Well," said I, "I suppose the longer we stay here the more exact will be our knowledge of this peculiar institution."

I had considered Egyplosis as a successful institution for developing the human soul. Certainly Harikar with his beloved attributes required a fit home for his complete development.

I had praised their oasis of love, of refinement, of rest, and of beauty, and even ventured to assert that such a paradise was the outcome of the love and purity of twin-souls. I forgot in my enthusiasm the possibility of the soul being satiated with pleasure, that life is a warfare ever seeking but never gaining repose, and that we are led more by our passions and illusions than our judgment. I forgot that while man resists pain he always yields to pleasure. I forgot that he was created for difficulty, which is the oxygen that feeds the flame of endeavor, and that difficulty alone can develop efforts which pleasure so easily destroys.

"I am of the opinion," said the doctor, "that this institution is founded on a perversion of human nature. This so-called hopeless love is, as we have just had proof, one of the most disturbing elements in life. Its victims resemble Tantalus, who, though steeped to the lips in water, can never drink. They are the unhappy devotees of an idol, and, like the Hindoos, stick into their sides the hooks of a cruel passion and swing aloft in torture to the applause of an admiring crowd."

"You evidently do not reverence hopeless love?" I remarked.

"I consider Egyplosis," he continued, "but a nervous asylum on a large scale. This nervous temperament, with its hysterical

raptures and tears, its painful sensibility, its exalted spiritualism
and irresistible sympathy, departs so far from the steady
temperate sphere of action that can alone sustain alike the
pleasures and disappointments of life as to become the object of
pity. These are the marks of a mental disease. Ultra-romantic
ideas and whimsical and unaccountable tastes are attributes of
this temperament. It is a kind of insanity, not the insanity
proceeding from hopeless mental aberration, but founded on a
systematic train of ideas born in a heated enthusiasm. It may
lead, however, to hopeless insanity."

"Doctor," said the astronomer, "you are taking a very
cold-blooded view of the subject. You seem not to have
discovered that the life here is ideal. From what you say one
would think that love is a species of insanity."

"That is precisely my idea," replied the doctor. "Haven't you
observed how foolishly people act when in love? All ordinary
human prudence and judgment are thrown aside. Love pares the
claws and pulls the teeth of man as a rational animal. Love is
supreme folly."

"I think," said the astronomer, "the climate of this country
has something to do with the present institution. You see that
the sun here never sets, and, were it not for his diminutive size,
would infallibly turn the entire interior world into a desert,
such as the moon is at present, where the outer sun's heat falls
for fourteen days on the one spot without intermission,
completely blasting her territories. The mild yet incessant heat
of Swang creates a fervor of blood and a romance of
temperament unknown in lands possessing night, hence the
practices of Egyplosis are a natural result of climatic conditions.
The appetite for ideal love has been created by the climate, and
the religion of the country very naturally responds to the
craving of such appetite. Who knows what excesses might not
obtain if no such restraint were imposed on the most gallant
youth of the country."

"I think," said the naturalist, "that the proper thing to do
would be to have their people imitate the conduct of Jacob of
old and Rachel. Jacob worshipped ideal love in the person of
Rachel for seven years and then married her. If our commander
would only propose such a scheme to the supreme goddess it
might possibly be favorably considered."

"Do you really suppose," said I, "that I possess any influence with the goddess, or that any recommendation of mine would be able to change the constitution of Atvatabar?''

"Well, sir," said he, "if you will allow me to make the remark, I think the supreme goddess takes quite as much interest in you as you do in her, and would treat your opinions with great respect.''

"You think more than I have ever dared to think," I replied, "and your thought savors of sacrilege. The goddess belongs to her faith, her country. To prefer an individual soul is to dethrone herself as goddess and meet a painful death.''

"In any case, whatever happens, you can rely on the fidelity of your followers," said the naturalist.

The subject was fast becoming embarrassing and I merely said: "Gentlemen, I am assured of your fidelity; so please let us dismiss the subject.''

The hour for rest having been sounded, I sought my couch, but not to sleep. The remarks made by my companions, emphasized by my growing fondness for the goddess, set me to thinking what the end would be of our discovery of Atvatabar. I wondered if Lyone was not, as sung by her devotees,

> "A chrysalis eager to hover
> And fly from her prison away.''

Could it be that the goddess might possibly, if an occasion worthy of such a step presented itself, fly from Egyplosis, renounce her throne, her crown, her sublime office of supreme goddess of Harikar, and with me retire to some far-off country, braving in the meantime the almost certain prospect of death. For her sake I felt I could meet any situation, however terrible, but for my sake would she throw aside her unparalleled dignities? Even if in trying to escape we outflew in my own vessel their ships of war, we could never escape the ubiquitous wayleals, the magnic-winged troops that could fight equally well on land or sea.

Bah! I said, such a dream is idiotic. When I thought of the splendor of the position that she would be obliged to renounce for the sake of her love for the passing stranger, and of the awful penalties that awaited transgression in one so exalted, I considered that no craving of passion should dare to resist such difficulties.

Here duty was resistance. Nowhere is man exonerated from the penalty of having to pay a price for his possessions, and even possession itself is not happiness. Better, I said to myself, to depart in peace than encourage the goddess in a desperate enterprise, if indeed she had any such desires as my vanity attributed to her.

CHAPTER XXXIV.

LYONE'S CONFESSION.

THE following day I again met the goddess in the same magnificent apartment in her palace. She was in a contemplative mood. A white robe of the finest silk enveloped her, showing to full advantage her superb figure. Her silky, shadowed eyes shone with a mild translucent light. The ripe beauty of her face was somewhat pale, for some tearful memory possessed her. Over her shoulders fell the torrent of her hair, while on her brow gleamed a diminutive diadem whose central part was fashioned like the throne of the gods. She wore a heavy necklace of shrimp-pink pearls.

As we reposed on wide, luxurious couches a maiden of rare beauty brought us dishes of curiously-prepared meats and wine of the finest vintage in flagons of gold. From distant cloisters came wafted the echoes of singing priestesses breathing their intoxicating Amens.

Lyone had been reciting her past soul experiences, now and then pausing as the story would grow more sacred. To me the revelations of the goddess were of breathless interest. I dare not urge her too forcibly, fearing to break the spell of her confessional mood.

She was pleased to say that my advent in Egyplosis had revived the past as no other event of late times had done. She was willing to recall the sweet experiences of her early life, prior to her elevation to the throne of the goddess.

I knew she was in that mood when confession to a kindred soul is most consoling to the heart. I urged her to continue the story.

"Well," she continued, "my parents, who were people of importance in Calnogor, had destined me for marriage and the outer world, but before I even knew of Egyplosis I had a day dream. I saw with my waking eyes this temple-palace as one might see it in a picture, splendid as the reality. I saw myself with a youth of noble aspect standing in a court of the garden, and his arm was around me. He was tall and shapely as a palm tree and was all tenderness and devotion. The picture vanished, yet its influence remained. It utterly transformed me from the undreaming girl that I was to a soul active and ardent, already experienced in what life really was. I learned that the mystery of life was love, and longed for spiritual companionship with an inmate of Egyplosis."

"Was the dream fulfilled as you expected it would be?" I inquired.

"Exactly as I anticipated," said Lyone. "I entered Egyplosis in spite of the earnest desire of my people to remain in the outer world and lead a life of barren conventionality."

"Had you not learned," I inquired, "that it was impossible to overleap the purposes of nature without paying a penalty therefor, that ideal passion will in time give way to the commonplace, just as water follows the law of gravity?"

"I knew nothing but that ideal love might be eternal. It is the passion that makes a goddess human and the mortal divine. Within a month after entering the temple walls I discovered the very reality of the image I had seen years before. He was my twin-soul, my lover, my god. At our first meeting we simultaneously burst into tears. It was an ecstasy in which the body did not participate to any marked extent, but belonged purely to the region of the soul. We accepted the vows made at the installation of a twin-soul and became a completed circle."

"Being the goddess," I said, "your lover must have died?"

"He died some years ago," she said, "and on his death, by reason of my widowhood, my gifts, my spirituality, my love and my beauty, I was elevated to the throne of the gods when vacant, and was worshipped as supreme goddess of the faith. It is utterly against our laws for a goddess to choose another counterpart; she is supposed to belong only to Harikar, the ideal soul whom also she symbolizes; hence I am obliged to dwell largely alone."

"You doubtless regret the loss of your earthly counterpart?"

I urged.

"Regret it! Ah, that was life!" she said, "for my soul then knew what spiritual freedom means. I experienced ecstatic agonies, bliss was pain and pain paradise. I flew as a bird full of anguish, bearing treasures of love and tears. I desired self-sacrifice, I wanted to smile on every one, to help every one. I loved life; I had no fear of death. My capacity for rapture seemed to expand continually. Every scene I gazed upon trembled in a new blaze of delight. Thoughts, like lightning, rent open new worlds of passion and tenderness, wherein I moved as a goddess peerless and supreme. But when the tomb closed upon my heart of hearts I begged them to lay me by his side and seal the door upon us forever. The glory of life had departed, and day after day I swooned upon the sarcophagus that held my treasure, my life."

Lyone was unusually excited, and to divert her attention from the past I spoke of the present, of her proud position as supreme goddess of Atvatabar.

"How does it affect you," I exclaimed, "to be the recipient of such adoration as you receive as goddess?"

"At first it was soul maddening," she replied; "I thought I should never be able to sustain such adoration. My soul, blinded and bewildered by the incense of song and prayer, seemed unable to bear the intoxication. Even yet, as I sit upon the throne of the gods, fantastic, astonishing emotions thrill me into swooning away. Oh, it is incomparably glorious to hear around you those earthquake surges of prayer, to see souls quivering with adoring love. I feel at times as though I were the cone of a volcano radiating fire and flame into a burning sky!

"Then, again, I smile, and feel as I smile that I have power over life and death — oh, you do not know what love is — you do not know its tremendous power until you feel its splendid flame breathed from ten thousand souls clasping your shrieking soul in a blood-crimson embrace! If thoughts be things it makes me a creator. If thoughts can chisel matter, then I am gracious in face and figure. Men say my flesh is smooth as marble, soft as velvet, and bright as gold, even as the forms of our priests and priestesses are sculptured and colored by the thoughts of love.

"Only a goddess knows such thoughts as hers that burn in the soul like fluid gold. Imagination fills me at times with vast and phantasmal splendors. Adoration glorifies me like light raining on the palms and palaces. I see shapes of burning sweetness, and the air around me is laden with the caresses of heavy, strange perfumes. Unclothed raptures, exquisitely soft and tender, surround me, like heaven opening its wings of flame upon the world. Happy voices, ringing in the sensuous arcades of music, fall on my ears, the blown spray of immortal friendships.

"Yet, is it not strange that all these delights, violent and glorious as they are, do not wholly satisfy the soul? I continually long for something sweeter yet. It seems the greater the joy the more enormous the capacity, and no joy completely fills the ever-expanding soul."

"You think," said I, "that even the rapture of a goddess is not wholly adequate to create a feeling of repletion of satisfaction in a soul such as yours?"

"It is contrary to our laws to think so, yet at times I know I could forego even the throne of the gods itself for the pure and intimate love of a counterpart soul."

"You are not so desirous of the human soul in its collective form as you are of individual soul wholly yours?" I ventured, shaken with a quivering thrill.

"The soul ever seeks that which is beyond and individual," said Lyone; "having once loved the individual soul, I know what such holy rapture means."

"What are the difficulties to be surmounted in your quest of a counterpart soul?" I inquired, with a secret delight.

"The sacrilege of a goddess becoming attached to the individual to the exclusion of all other individuals. The goddess-elect must have been a novitiate and priestess of Egyplosis and the survivor of her counterpart soul. Her experiences as a noble and pure priestess, together with special beauty and popularity, are the conditions for the peerless office of supreme goddess and incarnation of Harikar. By her vows she can never again become the exclusive possession of any one soul. She belongs to Harikar, the universal soul."

"And what is the punishment for renunciation of your office and attachment to another soul?"

"A shameful death by magnicity for the twin-soul. No goddess can resign her office. No goddess can seek a lover and live."

"Not even an ideal affinity?" I asked.

"Why, even ideal affinities who forget themselves are

punished with lifelong imprisonment, and their names blotted out of the priesthood as though they were dead," said Lyone.

"Are there many such transgressors of their vows in Egyplosis?" I inquired.

"There are, I believe, some five hundred twin-souls at present immured in the dungeons," said Lyone.

"Poor souls!" I murmured, "their apostacy was but their reformation."

"I often think of them," said Lyone, "but I know I can never liberate them except by my own successful apostacy. And yet when all else is peaceful and happy, or at least appears so, why should I become the leader of an insurrection that would precipitate a hundred times more misery on the nation, to say nothing of the possibility of defeat?"

I saw that a crisis had come to Lyone, a tremendous debate agitated her soul. I forebore treading further on the sacred ground. She, with true delicacy, was striving to hide the intensity of her proud unrest. I felt that in time she would have the courage to take the irrevocable step that led to freedom or death.

As I sat devouring every word spoken by Lyone I felt a strange power surrounding me, an emanation of the soul of my beloved friend. I resisted for a long time a sacrilegious desire to fling myself at her feet and clasp her in my arms. I thought of her supreme dignity, her love for her faith and her people, and I knew one cold glance from her eyes would pierce me through and through like a sword. The more I thought of my position at that moment the more amazed I became at the audacity that led me to ever think of claiming the soul of the goddess as mine, much less my encouragement of an enterprise so desperate as we had already assuredly embarked upon.

As I gazed in adoration at the splendid soul before me the scene through the open windows seemed to grow more ideal. There was a new glory in the gardens around me, a finer flashing of fountains in the sunlight, and a bolder chiselling of palaces and temples. Beyond and above there wheeled the roof of the world, with its still more prodigious forests and mountains and a wider expanse of gleaming seas.

I sprang forward with a cry of joy, falling at the feet of the goddess. I encircled her figure with my arms and held up my face to hers. Her kiss was a blinding whirlwind of flame and

Her kiss was a blinding whirlwind of flame and tears! It was the proclamation of war upon Atvatabar. Thenceforth we became a new and formidable twin-soul.

tears! Its silence was irresistible entreaty. It dissolved all other
interests like fire melting stubborn steel. It was the
proclamation of war upon Atvatabar! It was the destruction of
a unique civilization with all its appurtenances of hopeless love.
It was love defying death. Thenceforward we became a new and
formidable twin-soul!

CHAPTER XXXV.

OUR VISIT TO THE INFERNAL PALACE.

THE infernal palace was a congregation of subterranean
rock-hewn temples under the spiritual control of the grand
sorcerer Charka and the grand sorceress Zooly-Soase.

The grand sorcerer's dominion was directly underneath the
supernal palace of Egyplosis. An ornate pagoda of stone covered
the entrance to the underground palace. The descent was by
means of a wide gradient of polished marble, and there was also
an elevator car, beautifully decorated with electroplated sheets
of gold and lit by electricity, which was the most rapid means
of descent to the pavement beneath, a distance of two hundred
and fifty feet. The procession of twin-souls and attendants, who
carried Lyone and myself in a splendid litter of gold, entered
the palace by means of the inclined marble highway whose
sculptured walls were radiant with electric light. The many
temples of the underground palace were devoted to the most
occult worship of Harikar. There was an immense central edifice
whose roof, supported by lofty columns, and sculptured in
fantastic beauty, rose two hundred feet above the pavement.
Here electric suns lit up what was merely the vestibule of a
hundred temples all hewn from the same pale green marble, the
aquelium floors glimmering like a fathomless sea.

As we entered this splendid abode of sorcery, we were
received by the august officials of the sanctuary. The grand
sorcerer Charka was a man of imperial presence, gracious and
subtle. His flesh was of the hue of silver bronze and he
possessed noble features. His hair was blue and his blue beard
was trimmed into a rounded semi-circle on his chin, while his
mustache spread nobly on either side of his lips. He wore a robe
of emerald blue silk, embroidered with silver flowers. The grand

sorceress, Thoubool who accompanied him, possessed the complexion of a pearl, was arrayed in a robe of celestial blue silk, and, like the grand sorcerer, wore a diadem of rubies.

Our reception was extremely gracious, the grand sorcerer saying he felt highly honored with our visit.

As we passed down the palace pavement, an immense bell opened its mouth of gaunt and glorious bronze. Soft explosions of music swept in thrilling moans through temple and cloister, the echoing walls resounding with ritournels of enthusiastic peace. As if inspired with passion, I could hear the bell swing and roll on its delirious pivot uttering its deep-sounding fantasy.

I saw, illuminating the sculptured archway of each temple on either side of us, the name thereof in letters of incandescent light. I saw the names Amano, Biccano, Demano, Hirlano, Kilano, Pridano, Redolano, Ecthyano, Oxemano, Jiracano, Oirelano, Orphitano, Cedeshano, Padomano, Jocdilano, Nidialano, Bischomano, Omdolopano and many others, indicating the various departments of soul development to which each temple was dedicated.

The sorcerer waved his wand and suddenly a band of priestesses appeared on the pavement moving in strange and fantastic measures. Their attire consisted of low-cut circles of bright and beautiful stuffs with short skirts, having in front of each a sheaf of heavy folds that expanded and fell as the dancer moved. All wore jewels and rings of precious metals on wrists and ankles. Their faces, perfect in feature, were pale rose in color but marvellously delicate. Ranging themselves on either side of the immense aisle, they formed a delightful guard of honor for the grand sorcerer and his retinue.

They were not only souls, but the materializations of souls, that danced and sang as when on earth. They were souls of former priestesses reincarnated by the sorcerer and who vanished when we reached the entrance to the temple of the labyrinth. It certainly was a delicate and superexcited imagination that wrought the splendid archway through which we passed into the grotto garden beyond. Neither Greek nor Moor, Hindoo nor Goth ever conceived such arabesques as were sculptured on the walls of the entrance to the holy of holies.

In the garden, hewn from the solid stone, were interminable thickets and hedges enclosing labyrinthine walks. There were open spaces in which stood veritable trees with strangest leaf and flower, branch and stem delicately chiselled from the solid rock. There were also acres of grass and flowers, wonderful creations of art. There were rose bushes, heavy with their eternal bloom, the flowers stained crimson as in life and the leaves their varying gradations of green.

Fruit trees, with pale pink flowers and leaves light and dark green, stood amid the green grass that never waved in the breeze. An immovable streamlet ran down its bed of carved irregularities between flowery banks and underneath a bridge formed of a single arch.

I looked up expecting to see the sky, but my gaze met the solid heavens of stone, and I knew again I was in a cavern. The feeling was somewhat suffocating. The garden was lit by an electric sun in the centre of the roof two hundred feet overhead. The pathway, wide enough for six people abreast, led by labyrinthine dells to the pagoda of the sorcerer, which stood in the centre of the garden. The mazes of the pathway were so numerous that none save the initiated, when once in the labyrinth, could find their way out again.

It was a weird experience to find myself walking between the master twin-souls of that subterranean paradise, exploring its many mysteries.

We arrived in due time at the entrance to a mighty temple at the further side of the labyrinth, whose bronze door suddenly opened to receive us, and the sorcerer bade me enter.

Passing through a pillared porch we entered a wide and lofty space lit by tall windows and a roof of many-colored domes of glass that threw wonderful lights on the polished aquelium floors of the building. The light that shone through window and dome was produced by myriads of electric incandescent lamps that glowed in recesses of the rock behind each window. This was the inmost shrine of the sorcerer.

As I walked toward the centre of the mysterious temple the sorcerer inquired if creative magic was cultivated on the outer sphere.

I informed the sorcerer that necromancy, divination, magic, clairvoyance, esotericism, and theosophy were things known and practised in many countries. "But," I added, "the idea there is that of self-abnegation and miracles are only to be performed by ascetics who practise the most rigid austerities. Men who desire to possess occult power live in complete solitude, subjecting themselves to cruel mortifications. They abstrain from all fellowship with their kind, they try to live even without food. They absolutely mourn existence, avoiding all contact with everything earthly. They hope by renouncing all the actions of life to enter more and more into the spiritual existence. They believe they can build up an enormous soul out of the ruins of the body."

"Do you find that such a method produces a high development of creative power, love, justice, conscience, truth, temperance, order, and benevolence?" said the grand sorcerer.

"I cannot say," I replied, "that the devotees to whom I refer are conspicuous for those qualities, certainly not for a highly active state of such qualities. Their abnegation develops fanaticism, which is intemperance itself, and fills them with hate toward those outside their creed. The starvation of every appetite of pleasure withers up the appreciation for every form of human delight."

"Then what virtues are derived from ascetic practices?" inquired the sorcerer.

"Certain virtues of a negative order," I replied. "The adepts claim to have power to create and transport matter; a claim which reliable history does not, except in a few cases, recognize, and in a very limited sense they have power to separate the soul from the body. While the body remains in a comatose state, the soul traverses space, holds consultation with similar souls, and returns to its mansion in the body again."

"Your magicians," said the sorcerer, "weaken or kill the body without imparting corresponding power to the soul. Now we of Atvatabar believe that the body should be developed equally with the soul. We believe that contact with the noblest and best of earthly things develops power and beauty. We feed both body and soul on the perfection of things, that both may thereby absorb perfection. In the brilliant activities of the supernal palace, and in the golden calm of the infernal palace, priest and priestess, as twin souls, naturally intermingle in the enjoyment of a long Nirvana of ecstasy. We have not only the occult power to perform miracles like the ascetics of the outer sphere, but the soul possesses an enormous development of every noble quality without which our golden century is impossible. We are able by means of our baths of life to obtain a hundred years of glorious youth, during which period age and

decay of the body is suspended. Our devotees when they arrive
at the age of twenty years, when youth is fully developed, begin
their Nirvana of blessedness and love. They do not grow older
during these years. The eye is as bright, the pulse as bounding,
the heart as lively, the complexion as pure and lovely, the
feelings as fresh, at the end of the interregnum as at its
commencement. Then when the golden century is exhausted,
the body begins to be twenty-one years old."

"Do you mean that a man who has lived one hundred and
thirty years is but thirty years old?" I inquired.

"Precisely," said the sorcerer; "why should we call a period
age in which there is no change?"

"Do all souls live until their century of youth is
accomplished?"

"Not all souls. Many die of accident or in consequence of sin.
With some, Nirvana consists of but a single day's felicity, with
others a month, or a year, up to a hundred years. It is the ideal
for which we strive, and there is no reason why the body should
not live one thousand years as well as one hundred, when
vitality becomes more developed."

I was astonished at the remarks of the sorcerer, and yet I
remembered the case of Adam, Noah, and Methusaleh. I told
him that men on the outer sphere had lived almost one
thousand years.

"You may be sure they never practised the austerities of the
ascetic life you have just mentioned. They must have enjoyed
life always turning their faces to the sun."

"I think one hundred years a great step toward immortality,"
I remarked.

"At twenty years the body is developed, but even a hundred
thousand years will not develop the soul. Think of the
development involved in having power over disease and death,
power to create substantialities of matter!"

"Do you create matter?" I inquired breathlessly.

"I will show you what we can do," replied the sorcerer; "if
you will follow me."

The sorcerer led the way to seats upon a platform of silver,
on which stood in terrific grandeur the figure of a hehorrent, or
dragon of gold, whose eyes were blazing rubies. He stood before
the dragon, at least twenty feet above the pavement of the
palace.

The labyrinth was a subterranean garden, whose trees
and flowers were chiseled out of the living rock.

Presently the sorcerer shouted with a loud voice, "My host! my host!" and at once several thousand twin souls thronged into the immense temple, dancing with naked feet on the polished aquelium pavement. Beneath the monster miles of wire were wound in a coil, and to the wire were attached twenty thousand fine wires of terrelium, each wire terminating in a terrelium wand. These wires were held one each by priest and priestess, who began to move in a strange dance on the pavement and sing an anthem to Harikar. As they moved more and more rapidly the clamor of bells arose, and explosions of sound, like bullets rained upon drums, shook the building. In the semi-darkness the body of the hehorrent seemed to quiver, and, as I gazed, lo! a shower of blazing jewels issued from its mouth. There were emeralds, diamonds, sapphires, and rubies flung upon the pavement, scintillating with fire the colors of the stones themselves!

The sorcerer, waving his terrelium wand, shouted, "Hold! It is enough!" and the seance was at an end. He received the jewels that had been collected by his hierophants, and descending, offered me a splendid ruby as large as a hen's egg. I looked at him with awe, as I felt its size and weight. He simply said, "These jewels have been created by spirit power."

"Do you," I gasped, with a feeling of mingled exultance and fear, "do you create matter?"

"The abnegation of hopeless love is the source of the spirit power by which we create matter such as this," replied the sorcerer. "The twin-soul is the cell that generates the creative force."

"And can you create other matter than jewels?" I eagerly inquired.

The sorcerer gazed at Lyone for a moment, who had been strangely silent in the presence of her most powerful spiritual coadjutor, and then replied: "Yes, we can create all things if necessary. We can, for example, create islands in the sea, with mountains, forests, lakes, valleys, winding walks and thickets of flowers, palaces and pagodas."

I was breathless with excitement at such a reply. "Oh, that I could see such an island," I rejoined, "and tread, if but for a single hour, its ecstatic shores!"

"You can both see it and walk upon it, if the goddess so wills it," replied the sorcerer. "What is the command of your

As I gazed, lo! A shower of blazing jewels issued from the mouth of the Hehorrent.

holiness?" he inquired.

"I would like the commander to see Arjeels, if your priests and priestesses are willing to perform the necessarily arduous ritual involved in its creation," replied Lyone.

"My hierophants," replied the sorcerer, "are only too happy to serve their goddess at all times, and I will at once command them to prepare to execute the ritual for creating the magical island of Arjeels."

"Your devotion," said Lyone, "fills me with the purest joy."

As we conversed, the large ruby I held in my hand had grown considerably less in size, as though the elements of which it was composed had to a degree evaporated as unseen gases, so that in a short time the jewel might wholly disappear. The sorcerer, anticipating an inquiry as to its disappearance, stated that all objects created by spirit power could only be maintained in their full material splendor so long as they were sustained by the power that gave them birth. The creations were not additions to already existing elements; they were simply focalizations of matter from the elements of the surrounding world, held together by the force that withdrew them from their normal habitat as long as the spirit power remains supplied. The jewels would in a few hours cease to exist, because they were not enfolded with the power that produced them.

"As to your magical island," said I, addressing Lyone, one of whose titles was Princess of Arjeels, "where is your principality situated?"

"It is located anywhere in the wide sea," said Lyone.

"Do you mean to say," said I, "that Arjeels is not a real, veritable island of the ocean, but only a ghostly island, a mirage that retreats as we approach it, a phantasy of the imagination?"

"Arjeels is a real island, with real rocks and waterfalls, lakes and forests, birds and flowers. There is a real palace, and all the appurtenances of an ideal life. All this is a materialization of the ideal desires."

I was astonished at her reply. "Once called into being," I inquired, "how long can the island exist?"

"So long as the twin-souls support it by never-ceasing ecstasy, so long as they perform their magical dances on the aquelium floor of the temple of the dragon, holding in their hands the terrelium wands. Once the island becomes materialized it requires thousands of twin-souls to sustain and preserve its reality, and it only vanishes when the twin-souls are utterly weary of their ecstasy."

"And when the twin-souls grow weary of their joys, what becomes of the island and its glories?" I inquired.

"We can preserve the island for a long time," said the sorcerer, "by having fresh dancers take the place of those that are exhausted, but after the lapse of a month, or longer, when all are utterly vanquished with fatigue, the spirit power becomes exhausted and the island disappears upon the sea."

I rose and enthusiastically grasped the sorcerer by the hand. "Ah, dear sorcerer," said I, "will you show me this magical island?"

"The command of the Princess of Arjeels," he replied, "will be obeyed."

CHAPTER XXXVI.

ARJEELS.

I WAS full of impatience to witness the creation of the magical island, where with Lyone I might find ideal delight. It was necessary, however, for the grand sorcerer to make ample arrangements, not only for the generation of sufficient spirit force to create the island, but also a force sufficient for its continuance for an indefinite length of time. It was absolutely necessary that there should be a reserve force of ten thousand twin-souls to take the places of the original legion of souls, when they would become weary of their ecstatic labors. Only once before had Arjeels been created, and it was thought a most wonderful thing that the sorcerer could preserve its existence for a single day. Now it was contemplated to sustain the island for months, and this required a continuous as well as a lavish expenditure of spirit power.

The sorcerer had enlisted his full quota of twin-souls, and prepared them for their heroic duty. The terrelium wand held by each soul was connected with the wires of a helic having immense coils of terrelium, that held by a rampant hehorrent of gold, formed an immense spiritual battery in the centre of another subterranean temple. Wires led from the battery underground across Atvatabar to the city of Mylosis, on the seacoast most remote from Kioram, a thousand miles from Egyplosis. The sorcerer announced a few days after the visit to the infernal palace that he was ready to accompany us to Mylosis, whither the queen's golden yacht had been sent to meet us.

The aerial yacht of the goddess flew swiftly over Atvatabar, bearing the precious Lyone, the grand sorcerer Charka, and myself to the far seacoast, the first stage in our journey.

The brightly flashing seas, the rose-colored sun, and the transcendent concave of the earth encompassing us, with the near tropical splendor of the country, made a scene of long remembered joy. But these objects, so glorious in themselves, were made still more splendid by the love that reigned in the souls that contemplated them.

In due time we reached Mylosis, where we found the royal yacht and a reverent crowd of people awaiting us.

The sorcerer lost no time in connecting the subterranean wires with a cable of terrelium on board the yacht, and, this being done, we immediately set out to sea, followed by a crowd of pleasure ships, conveying a host of people anxious to witness the miracle about to be performed.

We anchored the yacht at a distance of fifty miles from the coast. The grand sorcerer, surrounded by his acolytes, held in his hand a thick rod of terrelium, the extreme end of the cable, whose further extremity was connected with the battery in the Temple of Reincarnation at Egyplosis. An exchange of messages along the wire informed us that the ten thousand twin-souls had already begun their dance of Pure Being upon the pavement of the greater temple. Immediately a stream of flame leaped from the end of the rod, like water spouting from a tube under enormous pressure.

"Now," said the sorcerer, "by virtue of the spirit power in this cable, what I will to exist, will exist. I will that the magical island of Arjeels shall rise above the waves."

"I wish the island," said Lyone, "to have an elevation of five thousand feet in the centre, and at an elevation of four thousand feet fill a crater of the mountain with a lake of cool water surrounded by aerial gardens, and on the shore place a palace of rose-colored marble, luxuriously furnished, with servants to wait upon us. All else may be according to your own fancy."

"As your majesty wishes," replied the sorcerer, and as he spoke, a high mountain rose instantly from the sea a mile away, creating enormous waves, that threatened the safety of the yacht and the congregated vessels. A feeling of awe silenced the host of spectators.

Instantly, as quickly as the sorcerer moved his wand, the mountains became clothed with forests, and high up on the shoulder of the central peak appeared a palace of rose-colored marble, whose supernatural architecture seemed a celestial dream. The island was thirty miles in length and about fifteen in width from immense cliffs, foaming water-falls flung themselves downward to the sea. Dazzled with their blinding beauty, we saw ravines engorged with flowers. In green and glorious blessedness the island lay before us, complete, like an enormous emerald in a setting of blue sea. We were so awestruck with the labors of the sorcerer, that it seemed a sacrilege to set foot on the miraculous shores of Arjeels.

At a sign from the sorcerer, the captain of the yacht fired one hundred guns, and the vessel moved toward the romantic island. We came close up to a white marble wharf, and Lyone and myself alighted upon the sacred retreat. Everything seemed so natural, that we could scarcely believe the solid rock to be sustained by self-sacrificing love.

The adorable sorcerer remained on board the vessel, as it was impossible for him to leave his post of duty for a moment, while the dazed yet happy inhabitants of Mylosis departed homeward in their vessels.

It was arranged that when the spirit power that sustained the island would become exhausted, owing to the utter weariness of the twin-souls, the firing of a gun on board the yacht would be a signal that Arjeels would disappear from upon the sea.

The moment both Lyone and myself stepped upon the magical soil we felt an instantaneous increase of health and vigor. We did not at first use our magnic wings for flight, but walked along paths that wound around the beach of golden sand, shaded by towering palms.

After remaining for a time on the margin of the sea we rose on our wings, and, like birds, encircled the island, rising ever higher until we alighted before the palace created for Lyone, a gem of the rosiest marble, covered with a dome of gold that

flashed around it the light of the sun. The architecture was
broad and heavy with splendid carvings, and surrounded by a
pillared portico. The palace stood on the shore of a beautiful
sheet of cool water; elsewhere its shores were thickly clothed
with tropic foliage and aerial gardens of the greatest beauty.

We had reached at last the holy of holies of ideal attainment,
a retreat of bewildering beauty. The weird and splendid
proportions of the palace, with its domes and towers
ornamented with sculptured arabesques, rising from the soft
waters of the lake, a veritable Fountain of Youth, all
surrounded by the green and gleaming forest and gardens
without end, filled our souls with a new rapture. Everything was
so perfect and peaceful, so rich with life and beauty, so fresh
añd sparkling, so unspeakably happy, that I said, "This is the
end of all toil and ambition, this is the perfect flower of life.
Here is the lake of immortality, and here the fabled gardens of
the Hesperides."

Rayoulb, the chamberlain of the palace, and his acolytes,
who received us, were also the product of spirit power, the
reincarnation of former inmates of Egyplosis. They awaited us
before the palace, announcing a feast had already been prepared
for us.

The interior of the palace revealed new wonders. Wide and
lofty chambers were hung, some with woven and painted
tapestries, and some plated with sheets of gold, illuminated by
electricity with many-colored designs in precious metal. Others
were decorated with tender and brilliant frescoes, in which the
transparent plaster seemed to hold in its depths the tones of
gold, of ultramarine and vermilion, in fabulous scenes. Woven
and painted tapestries clothed the walls of still other chambers,
representing in entrancing colors the most occult mysteries of
Egyplosis. The banqueting chamber had a dome of enamelled
glass, that softened the light with many a caressing color.
Procelain vases, gorgeous in depth and richness of color,
containing plants of the richest bloom, added to the apartment
their decorative grace. There were also an art gallery, a library,
and a museum of jewels.

On one side of the palace a square cloistered arcade
surrounded a marble court. In the centre of the court lay a
square pool of crystal water, whose basin had been chiselled out
of the solid rock. The pool was fed by a wide water-fall falling

"By virtue of the spirit power in this cable," said the
sorcerer, "I will that the magical island of Arjeels
shall rise above the waves."

down a precipice on the pavement. Here also were several pagodas containing chimes of bells and large oblong vases of stone filled with blooming flowers.

Amid such splendor I began to realize that love has the power of spiritualizing all things, of interfusing them with its own rapture. Under its flame all colors brighten, all movement becomes divine, all labor seems holy. The sea attains a deeper blue, the shores a brighter green, the beloved one becomes more beautiful, more delicate and supernatural. Love, indeed, is an ultramarine and ultramontane joy!

"This delight," said Lyone as she lay in her boudoir, plunged in delicious blessedness, "fills my soul with universal peace. Hitherto pained with the chagrin of life, I welcome this unwonted repose. Oh, I am supremely happy!"

"This expedition," I replied, "is not to observe the transit of Venus, but the possession of Venus, to weigh each other's souls and read the poetry written in every fold of the heart. It would be the perfection of life if such reality of the ideal could surround us forever, but in a world where the worm doth conquer, where the storm wastes the flower and herb, such felicity is purchased only by the sacrifice of ourselves or of others. But while it lasts let us prize its ineffable joy. Hitherto," I continued, "philosophy has said that if we do not want to be undeceived we should never visit the haunts of imagination, for the fruits thereof are ashes, but we will create a new philosophy, that will assert that the haunts of imagination are ideally real, that the veritable Fountain of Youth has been discovered, that Eldorado may be won."

The following day found us floating on the lake before the palace in a beautiful magnic boat. Musicians occupied a pagoda overlooking the lake, and made the air sweet with their music. The lake seemed to fill the crater of an extinct volcano, and miles away on its further shore rose the lofty precipices of a mountain crest. It was most delightful to float on its profound wave, at an elevation of four thousand feet, and yet see the sea beneath us, and we surrounded with all the glory of the interior world.

Birds, gorgeous as humming-birds, resplendent in burnished hues of purple, garnet, and green, would flash amid the flowers, or chase each other over the water. As for ourselves, we no longer feared our own holiest emotions. Our deepest feelings were then in the foreground. The mysterious carmine on the palpitating lips of Lyone was the symbol of a warm, delicate, superexcited soul.

Lyone grew day by day more and more beautiful. She resembled the color of a deep and mysterious gold. I crowned her brow with flowers and wreathed her azure hair with wistful daffodils.

Another day we rode on soul-created horses to discover the odoriferous retreats of the island. The pathways wound through flowery ravines, that looked out upon the sea. The sweet cool air that filled the splendid gloom of the palm woods seemed the essence of gladness. What glorious vistas opened amid the luminous green of the forest! The murmur of music filled the infinite ways of the island as our cavalcade wound round its peerless hills or plunged into its abysses of flowers. The spell of an ideal land was upon us, and we experienced sensations hitherto unfelt in life.

"This," said Lyone, "is the ideal climate. Everything has become transfigured; even the light of the sun is softer and more blessed."

"And the goddess of Atvatabar," I replied, "has become more delicate, more supernatural, and more holy."

The island was one vast garden of tropical fruits and flowers, without the malaria of decay. Everywhere nature, carefully assisted by art, assumed the rarest beauty. Everything that savored of ruin and decay was non-existent. There were no wild or poisonous animals. No deadly serpent was coiled upon the branches, nor did poisonous insects crawl on leaf or flower. Forests of trees of a strange tropical vegetation abounded. There were the fruha, resembling dates; the caspariba, resembling bananas; the dulra, resembling limes; the jackle, resembling lemons; the congol, resembling oranges; the velicac, resembling bread-fruits; the persar, resembling custard apples; the phyorbal, resembling cocoanuts; the gersin, resembling mangosteens; the huflar, resembling coffee; the solru, resembling plums; and presuveet, or tamarinds lining the route. Fruits such as the troupac, or citron; dewan, or guava; orogor, or mango; and ryeshmush, or plantain gleamed amid the embowering foliage, and gardens of squangs and the pineapples, aloes, nutmeg, cloves and spices of Atvatabar, were on every hand.

One day, when floating on the lake, we heard with surprise and infinite sadness the discharge of a gun, the signal that the island was at an end. Spreading our wings, we awaited the catastrophe.

Suddenly a roar of thunder startled us, and Arjeels, with its majestic cliffs, its green forests and rivers of flowers, fell in one dissolving crash, and faded from sight. The lake and boat fell from beneath us so rapidly, that we would have fallen headlong into the sea had not our wings saved us. There flowed where the island had stood a circular wave rushing to a focus. There was an upward spouting pillar of foam, and all again was placid sea!

We flew downward to where the yacht awaited us, and alighting on board, soon reached Mylosis.

CHAPTER XXXVII.

A REVELATION.

ALAS for the brevity of earthly joys! The noble priests and priestesses had made a heroic effort to sustain Arjeels, but a month's incessant labors had quite exhausted their powers, and the glorious island vanished, with all its ideal sweetness. As if to intensify our sadness, when we reached Egyplosis again, we found the high priest Hushnoly, impatiently awaiting our return to secretly report the proceedings of a late council of the king and government, held in the council chamber of Egyplosis.

I knew by the appearance of Hushnoly that something unusual had happened. He hesitated to unfold his secret until requested to do so by the goddess.

"It is a serious business," said Hushnoly, "and I have been commissioned by his majesty to know the full meaning of the step both your holiness and his excellency are about to take, and see if there is no possibility of averting the terrible calamity, that overhangs Egyplosis."

"Tell me," said Lyone to the high priest, "what the council has been discussing, and what it has determined upon."

"Your holiness," said he, "I should inform you that Koshnili, as chief minister of Atvatabar, has received a report from his winged spies, charged with the duty of watching the movements of his excellency and retinue ever since their arrival in Atvatabar. His duty made it necessary to discover the real object of the illustrious strangers in visiting our country, and consequently their actions have been carefully watched and reported."

"And of course," said I, "my constant association with the supreme goddess, has led Koshnili to suspect me of designs inimical to the welfare of the kingdom?"

"Listen to the report made by Koshnili," replied Hushnoly, who unrolled a document he held in his hand, and read as follows:

"*To His Majesty*, KING ALDEMEGRY BHOOLMAKAR, *of Atvatabar*, *greeting:* Your faithful minister begs to report that his private wayleals have followed his excellency, the alien commander, Lexington White, and followers from their arrival in Kioram until their reception at Egyplosis. The illustrious strangers, after landing on our soil, travelled by sacred locomotive from Kioram to Calnogor, and were there the guests of your majesty, after which they attended a feast of worship to the supreme goddess in the Bormidophia. The illustrious strangers were then received by her holiness in her palace of Tanje. While lingering here my wayleals, from the ramparts of the palace, saw his excellency the alien commander, in company with her holiness, enter the silver pleasure boat. Their long-continued interview in the palace garden testified that a mutual affinity had drawn the illustrious personages together. From later observation my faithful wayleals are convinced that in the palace garden of Tanje was begun the awful possibility of a twin soul of our deity, and the alien commander, and the consequent apostasy of the supreme goddess, and her renunciation of Harikar.

"My faithful wayleals further report that while travelling on the aerial ship from Calnogor to Egyplosis, they obtained further evidence of the consummation of a deific and alien twin soul. The principals sat apart from all others, on a seat at the prow of the vessel, and the report of their conversation will justify your majesty in believing that a sacrilegious twin soul already exists in defiance of civil and religious law, her holiness and the alien commander being the illustrious components.

"Awaiting the further commands of your majesty, I remain,
with profound veneration,
"Your majesty's faithful servant,
"KOSHNILI."

I gasped for breath at hearing so brutal a dissection of our
hearts. I was thunderstruck. I could only ask Hushnoly what he
had to say on the situation.

"That you love each other, I need not ask," said he; "that
may be taken for granted. But I might ask, do you each of you
fully recognize the position you stand in? Do you know that
your conduct menaces the throne of the gods itself? I can
understand the violence of love for a human soul in the breast
of the goddess, but what of her renunciation of Harikar?"

"If not already convinced," I said, "I think her holiness will
soon see that all this monstrous system of hopeless love is
totering on its throne. It is an artificial society, that must in
time, of its own accord, crumble to pieces."

"His majesty," said the high priest, "has departed with his
retinue to Calnogor, and has called a council of the government
to consider the situation. He held that the rank of the
individuals who have offended against the sacred code of
Atvatabar, and the monstrous impiety of the offence itself,
constitutes a subject worthy of the most serious consideration
of the government. His majesty was extremely angry on hearing
the report of Koshnili. He characterized your excellency's
conduct as unworthy of the hospitality you had received, and as
involving the ruin of both the supreme goddess and yourself."

"What did Koshnili say when presenting the report?" I
inquired.

"Koshnili said that the affections of their beloved goddess
had been withdrawn from their only legitimate object, Harikar
himself, and had been appropriated not even by a holy priest of
the temple, not even by an ordinary citizen, but worse than all,
by an infidel, a heathen, an adventurer and a stranger,
emanating from some *terra incognita* that might, owing to the
fatal discovery of Atvatabar, one day send its hordes to ravage
the country with fire and sword. The council," he continued,
"knew the penalty for such treachery and abuse of hospitality
on the part of a desperate and fanatical stranger, as well as such
apostasy on the part of the goddess. He demanded the

immediate arrest of the guilty parties. The king had sufficient evidence to convict and execute both individuals by reason of their high treason against both the government and faith of Atvatabar."

"Did the king approve of Koshnili's demand?" I inquired.

"His majesty," said Hushnoly, "said that a matter of such importance required the greatest circumspection. Her holiness was known to be the most pious and popular supreme goddess that had ever sat on the throne of the gods, and although it was evident she had insulted Harikar, still if the quiet expulsion of the strangers from Atvatabar soil would prevent further disgrace of their faith and country, he would prefer to issue a decree of expulsion, rather than a decree for the arrest of both commander and goddess. To reduce the possible calamity now overhanging the nation to the least possible proportions, it would be necessary to act at once, rather than to await the development of more complete evidence of affection between the guilty parties."

Admiral Jolar deprecated the violent measures advocated by Koshnili, and supported the idea of the king, to quietly expel the strangers. He said that if the decree of expulsion were intrusted to him, he would see that it was carried into effect without delay. The council could rely on the royal fleet doing its duty.

Koshnili was angry at his idea of immediate arrest not being acted upon. "Suppose these strangers," he said, refuse to leave, and being warned by your royal mandate so fortify themselves by stirring up an insurrection in favor of her holiness, that might ꞏpossibly defeat the royal arms, and, in the end, we ourselves be sacrificed by our present timid vacillation. The crisis is a serious one and demands a desperate remedy."

"The Governor Ladalmir," said Hushnoly, "rebutted the arguments of Koshnili. He pointed out that the laws of hospitality demanded that the strangers should receive consideration at the hands of the king, even if guilty. They might receive fair warning to depart, after which, if the commander prove contumacious, more stringent measures could be taken. Should the commander, in defiance of the royal mandate, endeavor to consolidate his affection for her holiness, doing further sacrilege to our faith, ecclesiastical law has the remedy of death for those who would dare dethrone our faith, and lead our beloved goddess to take the irrevocable step of abandonment of her supreme office. After considerable discussion, it was decided to act on the suggestion of his majesty the king, that without bringing the matter before the Borodemy, a decree of expulsion be handed Admiral Jolar, for execution on the parties to be expelled from the kingdom. The decree is already in the hands of Admiral Jolar for delivery to your excellency."

CHAPTER XXXVIII.

LYONE'S MANIFESTO TO KING AND PEOPLE.

"MIGHT I ask your holiness," said the high priest, "if you will really take so determined a step as that indicated by the action of the royal council? The thought of such a thing strikes me dumb with fear."

"Hushnoly," said Lyone, "I have ever found you faithful to my interests, and I will now confide in you my purposes. You are a man of wisdom, calm and conservative, and can rest happy in the possession of your counterpart soul. Your character has become moulded by your long novitiate until you have become a part of the institution itself. To think of any other state of things is to you an impossibility. On thousands of souls here, your inflexible laws have only developed a rebellious energy that will some day utterly destroy the fabric of Egyplosis. The true union of souls is not artificial restraint and the present calmness is only the pause that preludes the explosion."

"But do you, supreme goddess, indeed desire to leave us forever? Will you profane your holy office? Will you despoil the temple of ideal love?" said Hushnoly, with emotion.

"You think it monstrous," said Lyone, "that I should desire to uproot principles so fixed and permanent. You can judge, then, how fierce must be the passion that causes me to antagonize duty consecrated by the ties and memories of my holy office."

"To break away from a responsibility so supreme," I said, "argues alone an extraordinary force. Your very system creates just such a love as this. Here souls are required to meet in rapture, and yet to stand balanced, as it were, on the thin edge of naked swords, and fall neither this way nor that. The development of a purely romantic love effeminates the race. The example of Egyplosis if carried out universally would obliterate the nation in one generation. The nation is wiser than its creed. Let us therefore choose the wiser path."

"It was the dream of your noble parents," said Hushnoly to Lyone, "to see you supreme goddess of Egyplosis. When you obtained this peerless honor they died. Your mother, dying, implored you to remember your vows, and to be ever true to your high office. 'Love only duty,' was her last sigh. If you love aught else, there is but a cruel death for you, and your memory will be an everlasting disgrace. Will you, the ideal of hopeless love, be the first to prove faithless?"

"What you say is true," I said, replying for Lyone, "but what is duty? Lyone not only owes a duty to her office, but also to herself. Her duty to herself is to rise up and break down this monstrous environment that chains down her soul, and her duty to these ten thousand souls is to tell them that an institution that constantly antagonizes nature is immoral. Here refined souls," I continued, "seek the cloister, not for peace, but for ecstatic anguish. They love and weep, and thus agitated they grow at once weak and violent, and can never accommodate themselves to the serious purposes of life. Thus sacrificed on the altar of a false god, weary of a life of barren blessedness, you will discover, if you but seriously inquire into it, that this palace is purely a prison for thousands of noble souls."

As I spoke, Hushnoly clasped his head with his hands and groaned. "With the downfall of Egyplosis," he murmured, "farewell delights, farewell tendernesses, farewell mystical, chivalrous love!"

"Do not be so dejected," said Lyone; "your imagination gives you but a capricious view of the future, which will be even nobler than the past."

The high priest could hear no more, and left us seized with affright as to the future, and mourning the anticipated downfall of Egyplosis.

Lyone, far from exhibiting fear, grew enthusiastic over our projected *coup d'etat*, that would certainly, if successful, create an organic change in the constitution of the kingdom.

We discussed the situation at length, and determined to leave Egyplosis for Calnogor forthwith.

I could in some measure appreciate the struggle undergone by Lyone necessary to sever her forever from so ineffable a retreat. But passion was stronger than environment, and it was duly announced that the supreme goddess and the commander of the *Polar King* and their immediate followers would leave for Calnogor forthwith.

Our departure from Egyplosis was attended with impressive ceremonies, our journey to Calnogor being made in the aerial ship of the goddess.

On our arrival at Tanje we discovered that the king and government had held their council unknown to the people. We did not think it expedient either, just then, to make public the determination of the goddess. I ordered my officers and sailors to Kioram forthwith to take command of the *Polar King*. My instructions to Captain Wallace were to have the ship fully supplied with stores, and remove her from the basin where she lay into the outer harbor of Kioram, and there await further orders. After a considerable period of inactivity the ship's company were nothing loath to get on board again with the prospect of another voyage. I confided to the officers the possibility of our being engaged in hostile operations, and ordered the ship to be put in fighting trim without delay. The officers and men were tendered the dignity of riding to Kioram in the sacred locomotive, and their departure was made amid the enthusiasm of the populace.

As for myself, I remained at the palace of Tanje, the residence of the goddess, to assist Lyone in preparing her manifesto to the people.

It was a painful crisis for her, who was the symbol of ideal love, to be the first to renounce its delights for the sake of an every-day union with a beloved soul.

For days her decision trembled in the balance. Her avowal of being led captive by human love would be a national catastrophe. She trembled for her ten thousand devotees in Egyplosis. It seemed a cruel and heartless trampling under foot of throbbing hearts that were thrilling with faith in their goddess. When I saw Lyone prepared to abandon Egyplosis for my sake, when I knew she would forever resign that splendid throne swept by whirlwinds of adoration, for the sake of being

clasped to my heart, when I saw her risk even life itself for the
simple love of one adoring heart, I then knew what love really
was. It was, as Dante says,

"Joy past compare, gladness unutterable,
Exhaustless riches and unmeasured bliss."

At last the decision was made. Lyone had decided that the
ideal love of Egyplosis was only suited to disembodied spirits,
and not for those breathing elements of matter that are unable
to exist in the spiritual state.

The following was the text of her manifesto to the king,
Borodemy and people:

"The Avowal of LYONE, *Supreme Goddess of Atvatabar, Holy
Ruler of the palaces, Supernal and Infernal, of Egyplosis,
Queen of Magicians, Mother of Sorcerers, Princess of Arjeels,
etc., etc., to His Most Excellent Majesty* KING
ALDEMEGRY BHOOLMAKAR *and the People of
Atvatabar.*

"The supreme goddess presents her respectful salutations,
and desires to inform his majesty the king and the people that
her ardent soul, sensitive to the tender feelings of human
affection, desires to live no longer without a counterpart soul.
The love of ten thousand souls does not satisfy the craving for
the love of but one soul. She has been told to love Harikar the
unseen. She reaches out her lips, but they do not meet with
love's delirious kisses. Her heart, withering within her because
of soul loneliness, has taught her to seek liberty, to love the soul
of her choice.

"She resigns her seat on the throne of the gods, as goddess,
having discovered her counterpart soul.

"She hopes that reform and not destruction will guide the
king and his ministers in dealing with Egyplosis at this crisis.

"Given at her palace of Tanje in this, the eleventh year of her
deification as supreme goddess.

LYONE."

This memorial fell upon the people like a shell of terrorite.
No one had ever suspected the crisis was so real. The king had
lulled himself with the belief that, as my sailors had already
departed to embark on the *Polar King*, I would possibly quietly

follow them, and leave the country without his having the trouble of even asking me to go. The message of the goddess, however, opened his eyes to the true state of things, and I forthwith received the following decree from his majesty, at the hands of Jolar, admiral of the royal fleet:

"ALDEMEGRY BHOOLMAKAR, *King of Atvatabar, to His Excellency Lexington White, Commander of the ship Polar King, etc., etc., greeting:*

"It having come to our knowledge that you, the said Lexington White, have conceived an affection for the sacred person of our illustrious supreme goddess, Lyone, spouse of Harikar, holy ruler of Egyplosis, mother of sorcerers, etc., in defiance of our holy faith and laws of this our realm, and furthermore it having come to our knowledge that the said supreme goddess has so far forgotten her holy duty as to reciprocate your affection, be it known to you that the penalty prescribed by the laws of this our realm for your heinous offence (which is sacrilegious treason) is death by magnicity, for both guilty persons.

"To inform you of the law and the penalty for your crime, and to give you an opportunity of renouncing your affection for our supreme goddess, and for your immediate departure from the soil of Atvatabar, we send you this our decree, commanding you as follows: That you forthwith renounce your treasonable affection, love and interest in the personality of said supreme goddess. That you embark, together with your officers and seamen, on board your ship, the *Polar King,* within one week from date hereof, and forever leave our realm of Atvatabar and the surrounding seas thereof. You must not again return to this our realm in any manner whatsoever, or send messengers, or correspond or conspire with any inhabitant thereof, particularly with our said supreme goddess, under penalty of death, both for yourself and for your entire crew.

"Given at our palace in Calnogor, in this fifty-sixth year of our reign.

"ALDEMEGRY BHOOLMAKAR,
"King of Atvatabar."

I received the document from the hands of the admiral with deep respect, and requested him to assure his majesty King Aldemegry Bhoolmakar of my profound regard and deep gratitude for the hospitable reception we had received from his majesty and his people during our stay in the glorious kingdom of Atvatabar.

I stated that we were at present in the act of leaving their country on a voyage of further discovery, but could not say that we would not again return to Atvatabar. We should be most happy to obey the command of the king, but should we receive a message to return from the supreme goddess ere we left the interior world, we might possibly return, notwithstanding the royal command, and brave the wrath of his majesty.

"In that case," said the admiral, "it would be my duty to prevent you from landing on Atvatabar soil; and should you succeed in eluding the vigilance of the fleet, your apprehension and that of your people by his majesty's wayleals would mean the execution of your entire party. We are a proud nation, and our army and navy are invincible."

I thanked the admiral for his well-meant warning, whereupon he withdrew from the palace.

CHAPTER XXXIX.

THE CRISIS IN ATVATABAR.

THE manifesto of Lyone had precipitated an historic crisis in Atvatabar. The king awaited my leaving the country with the utmost impatience. He made every effort to prevent the news from reaching the public, hoping that when I took my departure the goddess would be amenable to the laws of the realm, and the faith be thus preserved.

The more that Lyone and myself discussed the situation, the more apparent it appeared that we could not now draw back from the position we had taken. It was absolutely necessary to provide a following in case the government attempted arrest, or the execution of either or both of us. Trusty messengers were despatched to the high priest, Hushnoly, the grand sorcerer,

Charka, the lord of art, Yermoul, and the other friends of
Lyone, informing them of the step she had taken, and asking
their support in case any violence were offered her.

I advised Lyone to have her agents collect and transmit to
Kioram all munitions of war. Some of the royal wayleals were
armed with spears, and others with swords and shields. All
battles were fought in the air, by reason of the wayleals being
able to fly, as their movement on wings was more rapid than
movement on foot.

As already stated, the ordinary spear of the king's wayleals
was very effective, by reason of its discharging a magnetic
current into the body, causing instant death. With a view of
arming the army of the goddess with a more potent weapon
than magnic spears, I quietly had agents purchase for immediate
transmission to Kioram vast quantities of iron, and the material
for making gunpowder, which happily existed in great
abundance in Atvatabar. My idea was to start a manufactory for
firearms, which were unknown to the interior world, and arm
every man with a magazine rifle — a portable mitrailleuse, in
fact.

While engaged in discussing the plan of defence with Lyone
the crisis was precipitated by the press of the country finding
out the *coup d'etat* of the goddess. With a view of placing the
government in the most favorable light before the people, the
chief organ of the king, *The Calnogor Jossidi*, published a fierce
editorial condemning the action of the goddess, and reviling
what it was pleased to call "the contumacious invader and
despoiler of Atvatabar." The article ran thus:

"IMPIOUS SACRILEGE!
"ASTOUNDING APOSTASY!
"THE SUPREME GODDESS REFUSES FURTHER WORSHIP,
AND HAS DEGRADED HERSELF BY SEEKING
MARRIAGE WITH AN ALIEN LOVER!
"WHAT IS FAITH, IF DECEIT BE OUR DEITY?

"The sweet, the noble, the pure, the exalted worship of holy
love, and of its hitherto most perfect symbol, the Goddess
Lyone, is threatened with extinction, if it be not entirely
destroyed. That sweet and perishable affection that fills the
breasts of lovers, which has been for ages conserved, expanded,

and wrought into an enduring fabric of religion in the sacred temple of Egyplosis, is about to utterly perish by a mad act of apostasy on the part of the deity herself. Whither now will tender and faithful hearts turn to find a refuge for all that makes the life glorious? Our ideal soul has sunk into degradation! She has flung herself from her proud and happy throne, wounding our faith with impious sacrilege!

"Never before in the history of the world has the treachery of a goddess been manifest; we have had occasion hitherto only to mourn the apostasy of the worshipper. Now what avails our worship, if the object of our adoration fails us in the hours of need? Who is to console the bereavement of millions, when his majesty the king and government, follow the iconoclasts with the sword of justice; no punishment is too severe for such perfidious workers of iniquity! Death on the magnic scaffold is the penalty for the infatuation of the goddess and her atheistic lover! Wanting both men and money, the standard of revolt will be brought down by the first blow, and his majesty's troops can be relied upon to bring the rebels to swift justice. Let them be covered with eternal infamy who will support this fearful apostasy!"

It became necessary for Lyone to publish the following manifesto to the nation, stating briefly the reasons that led to her renunciation of Harikar, to become the apostle of a new creed of one body and one soul:

"LYONE, *who has been until now Supreme Goddess of the faith of Harikar, to her faithful people, greeting:*
"I, who have been exalted to the high seat of honor on the throne of the gods, as the incarnation of the supreme soul, having received divine honors at your hands, desire at this crisis to make known to you the nature of the reform I seek to establish in the faith and worship of Atvatabar.

"I do not seek to annihilate your faith, with all its tender and memorable qualities. I simply seek to reform such religion, making it more natural, more holy. All things that exist do change; if they do not rise to greater glory, they must sink to profounder shame. I, who have been your goddess during a long and blessed Nirvana, know how much you love me. I know that round my throne a tempest of passion has swept for years, filling me with its ecstasy. But I hasten to tell you that the delights of Egyplosis have been purchased at a fearful price. The sacrifices of its priests and priestesses have proved to me that even the retreat of ideal love can be as inexorably cruel as the outer world. So harassing have been these sacrifices that some could not bear their burden, and at this moment five hundred twin souls are confined in the dungeons of Egyplosis because they transgressed the vows of their novitiate. Of what avail are tender, chivalrous delights, if nature, if reason, be outraged in producing them?

"Those who have remained steadfast to their vows, have grown sickly and morbid, feeding too long on fantastic ecstasies. Despondent and unreal in mind, delicate and nervous in body, they only appear rich and radiant in some brief ceremonial, while their every-day life is shuddering, tearful, and unstable, and utterly unfit to cope with the struggle of ordinary existence.

"Therefore it is that one moment of pleasure is purchased by whole days of pain, and the oscillation between such extremes racks and ruins the dearest souls.

"The motto of the new faith for Egyplosis, 'One Body and One Soul,' founded on the ordinary marriage rite, will restore to priest and priestess the steady and temperate possession of their souls which gives society that virile force necessary to its very existence.

"By the memory of our mutual love, I claim the support of my faithful priests and priestesses, worshippers and people, in the coming struggle.

"LYONE."

The manifesto of the goddess, published in all the papers of the kingdom, created a profound sensation. It was the first discovery to millions that their religion had been weighed and found wanting. Although many were aware of its excesses, they saw that, despite every regulation, the hornet was in possession of Hesperides, prepared to sting the hand that reached for the golden fruit.

They learned that passion led to agonized exaltation, and that the moral fibres of the soul became paralyzed by fierce temptation and inordinate spiritual delights. They saw that restraint of rapture and a more natural basis for the fellowship of the sexes were reforms imperatively needed, if the religion of Atvatabar were to remain an elevating and purifying force. Their creed must be reformed, both in faith and practice, and who so capable of introducing such a reform as Lyone herself?

The power of the deep-rooted conservatism of those who had nothing to gain by the change, the fear of the merchants that civil war meant their financial ruin, of a king jealous of his authority, and of the supremacy of existing laws, were the forces that would oppose the power of the goddess to carry out her reforms.

I began to accuse myself of being entirely responsible for all this disturbance in a peaceful country. Had I never discovered Atvatabar, Lyone might never have desired to disturb the existing order of things, but would have remained an agonized and crowned goddess, wedded only to Harikar, in a temple of eternal celibacy.

I knew, however, that all this was changed. I knew it by her sighs at our first meeting in the garden of Tanje, which, to remember, again and again made me thrill and shudder with joy.

CHAPTER XL.

MY DEPARTURE FROM THE PALACE OF TANJE.

THE week of grace allowed me to leave Atvatabar had already expired ere it had seriously occurred to me to actually leave the palace. The commotion in the nation consequent on the publication of the manifesto of king and goddess was so great, and the necessity of advising Lyone in the crisis so urgent, that I did not take leave of her until the time for my departure was exhausted. One thing that made me somewhat careless of arousing the royal danger was that the *Polar King* with her terrorite guns could command Kioram in spite of the royal fleet, although it numbered one hundred vessels. Fortunately the royal fleet had not yet learned the use of gunpowder, their guns being discharged with compressed air.

A despatch from Captain Wallace stated that the ship was lying in the outer harbor, well equipped either for a long voyage or probable hostilities.

With the view of allaying the excitement of the people, the

king published a statement that the alien commander and his retinue had been ordered to leave forthwith. As for Lyone, the crisis had in no wise terrified her; she felt assured, however, that "the beginning of the end had come."

"Are you not afraid of life-long imprisonment or death in case your cause has no supporters?" I asked.

"They can do me no harm," she replied, "for the entire priesthood of Egyplosis, the Art Palace of Gnaphasthasia, and thousands of sympathizers among the people themselves, will rally to my flag when the hour of danger comes."

"You can depend on my operations at sea," said I, "in your behalf. Although I have but a single vessel, I will fight the entire fleet of Atvatabar. One shell of terrorite has more power than a thousand of their guns. I will destroy Kioram, if need be, to bring the king to submission."

Before leaving Lyone, I drew up a plan of campaign for the coming struggle. Hushnoly, the high priest, although conservative as regards the affairs of the priesthood, was really a trusty friend of the goddess, and would assist the grand sorcerer in commanding a wing of the sacred army.

The liberated priests and priestesses would fight like lions for the cause for which they had been imprisoned. The palace of Gnaphasthasia would also furnish its battalions, led by Yermoul, lord of art. Then, among the fifty millions of people there were perhaps twenty millions in favor of reform, who would contribute a large army in support of Lyone.

"It is by no means certain that a civil war will take place, even to secure the proposed reform," said Lyone. "The people may leave it to the Borodemy and the law to settle the matter."

"And what would be the result in such a case?" I inquired.

"Well, if I persisted in my demands, and no insurrection took place," said Lyone, "the king might put me to death as the simplest way of ending the matter, and appoint another goddess in Egyplosis."

"They will never hurt a hair of your head while I live: I swear it!" said I, with considerable emphasis.

Lyone smiled at my enthusiasm, and refused to permit me to linger longer with her. We understood each other perfectly. I saw that when Lyone had once made up her mind on a certain course, there could be no retreat. She cared not any longer for a dead throne, for even the worship of the multitude could not feed her famished heart. She must have a beloved soul, consecrated to herself alone, between whom would vibrate the music of great thoughts and tender emotions.

Lyone had declared war upon hopeless love. This was a necessary consequence of her altered position. Egyplosis, founded on a brilliant theory, had in practice become a prison, and she must open the doors to let its prisoners free.

Just as I was leaving the palace I received a message from Hushnoly stating that the king had secretly ordered my arrest, and to be circumspect if I wished to reach Kioram free.

Attended by a guard of bockhockids faithful to Lyone I set out for Kioram, taking a circuitous road to avoid Calnogor. I had been informed by Hushnoly that mobs of excited and bloodthirsty wayleals were flying about the metropolis, shouting "Death to the foreigners!" Mounted on a magnificent, majestic steed of great power, I led my little band at a furious pace. The bockhockids with each stride of the leg covered a distance of sixty feet, and could travel easily seventy miles an hour without appearing to run very quickly.

About an hour's travelling brought us abreast of Calnogor, and soon afterward I heard shots fired and the noise of a conflict. Making an aerial *detour*, I discovered a combat between a dozen wayleals on the one side and a crowd of wayleals on the other. I noticed that as fast as the individuals of the larger body were fired at by a weapon in the hands of the smaller company they at once became lifeless, either falling to the ground or hanging limp in the air supported by their still vibrating wings. Being intensely curious to see the wayleals using revolvers, I ventured with my men nearer the *melee*, and coming near the flying warriors, I discovered to my surprise and horror that the smaller band of flying men was a company of my own sailors, led by Flathootly, fighting back to back a swarming mass of wayleals.

The brave fellows fought like lions. No sooner did a wayleal approach a sailor with his deadly spear than he was shot. My men, fighting such fearful odds, for the enemy numbered several hundreds, could not long maintain so unequal a combat, notwithstanding the superiority of their weapons. It was only a question of time when their ammunition would be exhausted, and their spears would then be their only weapon, and I had evidently arrived in time to relieve them. Flathootly was

shouting to the enemy, "Shtand back, or Oi'll shoot yez!" when
I approached. The sailors cheered to see me flying to their
relief, and at that moment the enemy, recognizing in me the
very man they wanted, swarmed around to prevent my escape.
My bockhockids drew their spears, and the sailors used their
revolvers freely, and forming a flying ring, effectually protected
me from the onslaught of the king's wayleals. I rallied my entire
company, who received the rush of the wayleals with a
discharge of revolvers and magnic spears, by means of which we
killed several. Again and again the enemy fell upon us with
renewed fury, shouting their war-cry of "Bhoolmakar!" They
evidently meant to harass us until re-enforced by a detachment
of the royal troops strong enough to capture us.

A wayleal, in an unguarded moment, struck me on the
shoulder, fortunately with only one point of his spear, drawing
blood. Flathootly, who saw the blow, emptied his revolver in
his breast, and he fell to earth a dead man. I was surprised that
the enemy had not already annihilated my men, for,
notwithstanding their fear of the sailors' revolvers, three of the
sailors had been killed. It was terrible news to think of my brave
fellows being slaughtered, but I was determined to have revenge.
I singled out Gossody, the leader of the wayleals, and rushing
forward on my bockhockid, aimed at his head with my revolver,
and instantly killed him. The death of their leader paralyzed the
wayleals for a time. Before they could recover from their
surprise, we killed a number of them. The enemy, once more
rallying, made a fresh attack. They hoped to either kill or
capture us by sheer force of superior numbers. We killed dozens
of them, but at a fearful cost. Six of the bockhockids and three
more of our own sailors bit the dust. It was quite evident that it
would be only a question of time before we would be
completely annihilated. I saw that it was necessary for us to
reach Kioram without further fighting. We could not afford to
risk the life of another man, even to gain a complete victory. I
therefore ordered a flying retreat. The bockhockids were
arranged in a circle, in the midst of which flew our sailors. We
struck out for Kioram with the speed of the wind, pursued by
an ever-increasing horde of wayleals thirsting for our blood.
Such was our speed of motion that the thrusts of the enemy
were ineffectual. It was a magnificent sight to see the giant
machines, like flying cranes, devouring distance with their

wings, each ridden by a winged warrior. Wearied and exhausted with our fight, and still longer period of flight, it was a welcome sight to see beneath us the city of Kioram, and the *Polar King* riding at anchor in the outer harbor, beyond which lay the royal navy of Atvatabar.

When within sight of the city the enemy unexpectedly gave up the chase, and did not follow us further. We soon gained the ship, and in a short time our bockhockids decorated the masts and rigging. The story of my imprisonment and the massacre of the six sailors of the force sent to escort me to Kioram was soon told, and a more determined crew never trod the deck of ship of war. We would teach Bhoolmakar a lesson he would never forget!

CHAPTER XLI.

WE ARE ATTACKED BY THE ENEMY.

CAPTAIN WALLACE and the entire ship's company were overjoyed at my escape from the clutches of the enemy. The loss of six of our brave sailors was a terrible calamity in any case, but still more so in view of the impending attack by the enemy's navy.

We had a good stock of gunpowder on board, and the ship's mechanics under Professor Rackiron began the construction of a series of machine guns, each weapon having one hundred rifled barrels arranged in circles around the central tube. Twenty-five of these guns were constructed. To each tube was fitted a magazine, with automatic attachment, so that one man could handle each weapon, that would throw five hundred balls with each charge of the magazine.

The fletyemings of the royal navy possessed the advantage of numbers and ships, so that it was necessary for us to have the advantage in point of arms. Our monster terrorite gun and the terrorite battery gave us also an immense advantage over the gunpowder batteries of the enemy. Thus equipped, we were more than a match for any ten ships of the enemy. But when we saw one hundred vessels, the smallest of which was as large as our own, and many twice our size, bearing down upon us in battle array, we felt our chances of escape, not to mention victory, were hardly worth calculating.

It was a splendid scene for a naval battle. The harbor of Kioram was a bay fully fifty miles in diameter, and here lay the royal fleet, whose hulls of gleaming gold shone on the blue water, while beyond rose the brilliant whiteness of the sculptured city.

Captain Wallace had the ship ready for action. Every soul knew it was a life-and-death struggle. The sailors knew that success meant wealth beyond the dreams of avarice. For myself, the prize was something more worthy of our desperate courage — it was the priceless Lyone, possessed of a divine personality. Her life, like my own, hung in the balance. Should I win the battle, we would win each other. Should I fail to conquer, there was but one kind of defeat, and that was death.

Every man stood at his post in silence. Flathootly had command of a company of sailors. Professor Rackiron superintended our chief arm of defence, the terrorite guns — weapons, like our revolvers, fortunately unknown in Atvatabar. We had a large quantity of explosive terrorite on board, in the shape of shells for our guns. The shells contained each the equivalent of 100 pounds of terrorite — that is to say, they would each weigh 100 pounds on the outer earth, while the shells of the giant gun weighed 250 pounds each. The iron hurricane-deck, that did us such service in the polar climate, was put up overhead, as a protection from the onslaught of a boarding crew.

The ships of the enemy advanced proudly in a double line of battle. On the peak of each floated the ensign of Atvatabar, a red sun surrounded by a wide circle of green, on a blue field.

On the *Polar King* floated the flag of the goddess, a figure of the throne of the gods in gold, on a purple ground.

When but a mile off, we could see the guns on every ship pointed and ready for the attack. The enemy suddenly broke into the form of a semi-circle. It was the design of Admiral Jolar to surround us and capture or destroy the *Polar King* by sheer force of numbers. We allowed the formation to proceed, until the entire navy of Atvatabar surrounded us in an enormous circle.

Having executed this manoeuvre, a boat put away from the admiral's ship and approached us. In a short time it reached our vessel, and the captain of the admiral's ship, with several officers, came on board.

The captain demanded my unconditional surrender, "in the name of his Majesty King Aldemegry Bhoolmakar of Atvatabar." I had been declared "an enemy of the country, a violator of its most sacred laws, a heretic in active destruction of its holy faith, and a fugitive from justice." The captain, as the emissary of the admiral, demanded the immediate surrender of myself and entire company.

I asked my men if they were prepared to surrender themselves to the enemy. Their fearful shout of "Never!" disturbed the silence of the sea, and must have been heard by the distant enemy.

"You hear the reply of my men," I said to the captain. "Tell your admiral that the commander of the *Polar King* declines to surrender."

"Then," said the captain, "we will open fire upon you at once. We mean to have you dead or alive."

"Give the admiral my compliments," said I, "and tell him to open the fight as soon as he likes."

The captain and his staff rapidly disappeared, and we knew that the fight was certain. The officers had no sooner reached the admiral's ship than a report was heard; and a ball of metal crashed upon the hurricane-deck overhead, tearing a large hole in it, and then plunged into the sea. This was the signal of war. Before we could reply, the *Polar King* was the target of a general bombardment from all points of the compass. The balls that struck us were of different kinds of metal — lead, zinc, iron, and even gold. Although the range of their guns was accurate, yet, owing to the loss of gravity, the shots had but little effect on the plating of the vessel. Some of the sailors were severely wounded by being struck in the limbs with the large missiles hurled upon us, and I saw that if the enemy couldn't sink the *Polar King* they could at least kill us, which was even worse.

I gave orders to Professor Rackiron to train the giant gun on the admiral's vessel. The discharge was accompanied by a slight flash, without smoke, and we saw the deadly messenger make its aerial flight straight toward the admiral's vessel. It entered the water right in front of the ship, and in another instant an extraordinary scene was witnessed. The ship, in company with a vast volume of water, sprang into the air to a great height, with an immense hole blown in the botom of the hull. Falling again, she sank with all of the crew who did not manage to fly clear of her rigging. After the vessel disappeared, the last of the waterspout fell upon the boiling sea.

It was a great surprise to the enemy to see their best ship destroyed at a single blow. The effect of our shot completely paralyzed the foe for the moment, for every vessel ceased firing at us. At first it was thought that the admiral had gone down with his vessel, and until a new admiral was in command the battle would be suspended.

During the confusion we ran the *Polar King* through the breach made in the circle of the enemy, keeping his ships on one side of us. I determined to try the tactics of rapid movement, with the steady discharge of the terrorite gun, hoping to destroy a ship at every blow.

It soon appeared that Admiral Jolar was still alive, he having escaped from his ship in mid air, with his staff and a number of fletyemings, by means of their electric wings. He had alighted on the ship of the rear admiral, where he hoisted the pennant of the admiral.

The enemy was now thoroughly alive to the necessity of destroying or capturing us. I saw it was a mistake in allowing ourselves to be surrounded in a bay only fifty miles wide. To fight so many ships required ample sea-room, to avoid the possibility of being captured.

The admiral sent ten ships to guard the mouth of the bay. It was a satisfaction to know that the torpedo was also unknown in Atvatabar, else our career would have been cut short. The *Polar King*, running twenty-five miles an hour, was followed by the enemy's fleet, which, although slower in movement, had the advantage in numbers and could possibly drive us upon the shore. After sailing as far east as we cared to go, the *Polar King* lay to, awaiting a renewal of the battle.

CHAPTER XLII.

THE BATTLE CONTINUED.

THE royal fleet formed a wide semi-circle a mile off, and reopened its guns upon us. An unlucky shot struck one of our seamen and cut off his head. A perfect storm of shot rained upon us, so destroying our hurricane-deck that it was no longer of any protection to us. The enemy, encouraged by their success, closed in upon us. What we feared most of all was an attack by the wing-jackets, against whom neither our heavy guns nor superior speed would much avail.

Professor Rackiron aimed the giant gun right in the centre of the enemy's line of battle. The shell struck the middle ship and exploded. All three vessels were scattered half a mile apart, and made complete wrecks. The *Polar King* darted forward to pass through the breach made in the enemy, seeing our move, closed the gap in front of us. The ships ahead would have barred the way, but to prevent their doing so, we threw a shell of terrorite over the bow of the ship into the water. The sea rose on either side fully half a mile into the air, in solid pillars of water. In the confusion, we burst through the ranks of the enemy and were once more in open water.

The admiral must have been exasperated at our escape. He followed us as before, in close rank, firing as he came. We now saw that he was about to change his mode of attack, for, hovering in the air, a rapidly-growing swarm of fletyemings were preparing to give us a hand-to-hand combat. Each vessel furnished a certain contingent to the attacking force, until the aerial battalion numbered about five thousand men. Our position seemed hopeless. What could less than eighty men do against a host of ten thousand? At close quarters our terrorite guns would be useless.

With loud yells the fletyemings swept down upon us. Fearing our guns, they kept open rank and spread around the ship. Aiming at the densest part of the enemy, we destroyed about five hundred of them, but, quickly rallying again, they were upon us.

We were ready for them. Our battery of twelve terrorite guns, including the magazine guns and musketry, rang out a terrible discharge. Under the withering fire and fearful explosions our foes fell back, and the sea around was strewn with dead and wounded bodies. Luckily for us, the only weapons possessed by the enemy were their magnic spears. The wing-jackets, rallying again, swarmed upon the rigging and covered the ship like a cloud of vultures. Ere we could again discharge our guns, several of our men were beaten down by sheer force of numbers. They made splendid use of their deadly spears. The ship's crew, reattacked between the discharges of the guns, were many of them stunned and killed — the enemy after each discharge renewing the attack, being constantly re-enforced from the fleet. It was possible that we would be conquered by the fearful odds against us.

Our ability to keep up a fire from our guns grew more and more difficult, owing to the incessant attacks of the enemy and the vast accumulation of their dead bodies on deck. The spears of our foes were more formidable weapons than we had supposed, for their touch was death. It was evident, notwithstanding the carnage, that our men would be obliged to surrender, owing to sheer exhaustion. As soon as a wing-jacket dropped from the ranks of the enemy another took his place; our guns covered the sea with their dead bodies. The admiral was determined to conquer us at any cost, for he rightly surmised our victory would be a terrible blow to Atvatabar.

To remove ourselves as far from the fleet as possible, I directed the ship at full speed ahead for the outer water. The ten ships that lay across the entrance to the harbor would have to be destroyed, notwithstanding the ceaseless attack of the fletyemings, who followed our every movement. We acted solely on the defensive, and managed, while repelling the most furious onslaughts, to throw overboard the dead bodies of the enemy.

In the midst of constant fighting we managed to get the terrorite guns into position again, and when within a mile of the blockade fired the entire battery into it. Our shells sank every vessel they struck and broke several others from their moorings. Several more shots destroyed the remaining vessels, but only leaving their crews like a swarm of hornets free to attack us. This, however, was a minor matter compared with possessing the freedom of the outer sea. We rushed over the spot where the ships had been anchored, and soon left the pursuing fleet far behind.

The wing-jackets, re-enforced by the crews of the blockading fleet, renewed their attack. Having learned the terrible power of our magazine guns, they contented themselves with making attacks on unguarded points. But fifty sailors were thus engaged, while the remainder of the ship's crew, including the officers, worked the guns with a will. The revolvers of the

enemy disabled us considerably, but by firing our magazine
guns in every direction we kept the ranks of the flying enemy
pretty well thinned out.

Our tactics were to keep the foe divided, if possible, and
destroy the attacking force in detail. So long as the sailors could
stand by their guns we were safe. We could outstrip the fleet in
speed, thus reducing the chances of our immediate antagonists
being re-enforced, for those who at first attacked us melted
rapidly before the withering fire of our batteries.

Finding themselves unable to secure the ship, even with such
enormous sacrifice of life, the fletyemings suddenly retreated to
the fleet, leaving us free to rest ourselves and look after the
wounded.

The terrible strain of the fight had utterly exhausted the
sailors, who had fought for fifty consecutive hours, without rest
or refreshment. We tumbled overboard the dead bodies of the
enemy who had fallen upon the deck, and buried eight of our
own sailors who had been also killed. Several men were
wounded about the head and neck with spear-thrusts that had
failed to kill, but none seriously. Captain Wallace got an ugly
wound in his neck, but it was not sufficient to keep him from
duty. Flathootly, in slaying a fletyeming, received a wound in
the hand that required the attention of the doctor. Professor
Rackiron and Astronomer Starbottle passed through the fight
unscathed, while Professor Goldrock suffered from a broken
leg. Our helmets, provided originally for triumphal purposes,
had proved of the greatest possible value, and saved many a life
on board the *Polar King*.

All this time we lay in full view of both the enemy's fleet and
the entire kingdom. It seemed to us a strange thing that the
admiral did not continue the fight with his reserve of
fletyemings, who could easily outstrip the ship in their flight.
He still possessed thousands of wing-jackets who had never been
engaged in actual conflict, who might have relieved their
exhausted comrades and in time have forced us to surrender.

Was the supine conduct of the admiral caused by a panic at
our power of havoc or, did he think my retreat to sea really an
effort to escape the country?

If his truce was caused by a belief that he was unable to cope
with us he might have called the wayleals of the king to his
assistance, but possibly the pride of the service prevented an

alliance with the army for naval conquest, more particularly
where the naval forces outnumbered the enemy two hundred
to one.

The scene of battle lay in full view of the entire nation, just
as the kingdom lay in full view of ourselves. The nearer
inhabitants could see the movements of the ships and the
sailors, and the progress of the battle, so far, was known to
every one. If the impression was favorable to the *Polar King*,
doubtless there would be a demonstration in favor of the
goddess; if not, it would be because the capture of our ship was
considered certain.

We lay to, at a distance of ten miles from the enemy's fleet,
awaiting the renewal of hostilities.

CHAPTER XLIII.

VICTORY.

THE enemy, finding we were not disposed to leave
Atvatabar, began to move down upon us once more in battle
array. The royal fleet consisted of seventy ships, the former
thirty having been either sunk or disabled by us. As for
ourselves, the hurricane-deck, masts and rigging had been
hammered to pieces, but the hull was sound, the sailors
enthusiastic, and the terrorite guns unharmed and our spears
invincible.

As the enemy approached us their ships began to move wider
apart, with a view no doubt of circumnavigating us, and then
close in upon the *Polar King* as before. Another squeeze of this
kind might prove fatal, consequently our plan was to keep the
enemy at a safe distance and on one side of us, and destroy his
ships one by one with our guns while out of range of his fire, if
possible.

The admiral did us the favor of keeping around his ship half a
dozen vessels by way of protection, and in this manner drew
near. We were determined to bring the engagement to a close as
soon as possible by striking the enemy a terrible blow. As soon
as their vessels drew within range we struck the central group
with a shell from the giant gun. The explosion worked a
tremendous havoc among the congregated vessels, but without

waiting to learn its full effect I ordered twenty shells to be fired into the central mass in quick succession.

The result was appalling. The great want of gravity caused a vast irregular mountain of ships and water to be piled high in the air. We could hear the shrieks of drowning and dismembered fletyemings. Volumes of water shot to tremendous heights, became detached from the main mass, and floated in the air for a time in liquid globes.

It was some time before the whirl of wrecked ships and angry water, filled with perhaps thousands of wing-jackets, subsided to the level of the ocean again. The ships sank beneath the water, on which floated hundreds of dead bodies. Those fletyemings who had escaped accident or death, headed by Admiral Jolar, who was still alive, formed themselves into a compact mass as they hovered over the scene of the disaster for a final hand-to-hand attack. Re-enforced by thousands of fletyemings from the then unharmed vessels, they approached with yells of "Bhoolmakar!" Finding their ships useless, they were determined to fling themselves in heroic sacrifice upon us in such numbers as to crush us.

This was precisely their most dangerous form of attack, but we could only await their coming. As the living mass of men approached we saluted them with another discharge of shells, which exploded in the very heart of the unfortunate host. The carnage was dreadful, and hundreds of dead bodies fell into the sea. Admiral Jolar was killed, and without their leader the fletyemings became demoralized. Ere they could rally again, we were about to fire another round of shells, when Rear Admiral Gerolio, with a few fletyemings, left the main mass under a flag of truce and approached us.

We were nothing loath to receive their message. Alighting on deck, the rear admiral informed me that owing to the loss of their admiral they were disposed to cease fighting provided I would leave the country forthwith.

"Then," said I, "you wish to report that you defeated us by driving us from the country?"

"I shall report that it was a mutual cessation of hostilities," said he.

"It has cost us too much to give up the fight now," I said. "One of us must surrender."

"Do you surrender, then, to His Majesty Aldemegry

Bhoolmakar, King of Atvatabar?'' eagerly inquired the rear admiral.

"Do you surrender to Her Majesty Lyone, Queen of Atvatabar?" I replied.

"We make no such surrender," said he, very much surprised to know that Lyone had been proclaimed queen. "If we cannot conquer you by force of arms we have ships enough to starve you into submission."

"We care nothing for your ships," I replied, "we will destroy them one by one."

"You may sink our ships," said the rear admiral, "but you will never conquer our fletyemings. We will begin a hand-to-hand conflict that will not cease until you and your entire crew are killed or are our prisoners."

"The truce is at an end," I replied. "Return to your ships immediately."

The rear-admiral and his staff rose on their wings, and in a short time regained the cloud of naval warriors that hung in the air half a mile away.

During the truce the ships of the enemy had drawn nearer and at once opened fire upon us.

A well-aimed shot struck us under the water-line, penetrating our armor, and going clean through the side of the vessel. The central compartment rapidly filled with water. It was a fatal blow, for although the fore and aft compartments would keep the ship from sinking, yet it soon put out our boiler fires and left us a helpless hulk upon the water. The main deck, containing our terrorite guns, was on a level with the water, and a quantity of terrorite and gunpowder rendered useless. We were in a terrible position, for our small stock of available ammunition would be soon exhausted. The enemy soon discovered the effect of their blow, and closed around us like vultures hastening to their prey. We suffered a terrible bombardment, that killed more of our men, and finally the fletyemings closed around us in swarms to annihilate us.

Resolved to sell our lives dearly, we received them with a discharge of our magazine guns. They quickly rallied and renewed their attack, but as long as our ammunition lasted were afraid to come to close quarters. At last we drew our revolvers and the hand-to-hand conflict began. Some of the sailors used their cutlasses with good effect. We had proof that the magnetic spears in close quarters were terrible weapons. As I saw my men falling around me I felt that the game was up. I thought of Lyone, and the thought would not let me surrender. I was already wounded in the shoulder and body, and stunned, while the enemy was swarming in greater numbers than ever. Must we surrender?

Suddenly, at that moment, a shell came screaming through the air and exploded above the ship, right among the wayleals, killing twenty or more.

Merciful heavens! Can the enemy, after all, fire shells at us? But why use them when the fight is practically over, and why fire them among his own wayleals? Another and another shell exploded among the wayleals around us, and finally a regular tornado of them exploded all around the *Polar King*, putting the enemy completely to flight.

As soon as the air was cleared around us, I saw to my intense astonishment two friendly vessels, one of which bore the flag of the United States and the other the flag of England, firing shells at the enemy. I then knew the cause of our deliverance, and shouted for joy. My men — all that were alive — rose and cheered our comrades from the outer world! The excitement was overpowering! We could only, amid tears of joy, salute them and signal them to keep up the fight. We were saved!

A well-aimed shot from the Englishman sank still another vessel. This fresh disaster received from the strangers seemed to completely unnerve the enemy, for, strange to say, every ship afloat struck its colors in surrender! It was well that the rear-admiral did so, for it would have been only a question of time until his whole fleet would have been destroyed.

The fletyemings retreated to their ships, and in a short time the gold-plated ship of Rear-Admiral Gerolio, under the flag of truce, came alongside our vessel. The rear-admiral and his staff came on board, and delivered up his sword in token of surrender.

"You surrender to me as admiral of Her Majesty Lyone, Queen of Atvatabar?" I said.

"I do," said the rear-admiral, "and am willing to devote my services to the cause of her majesty."

"Will your fletyemings as well as yourself swear allegiance to Queen Lyone and her cause?"

"We swear it!" yelled the fletyemings of the rear-admiral's

ship, and, at a signal from their leader, the flag of the new queen took the place of the flag of his deposed majesty, King Aldemegry Bhoolmaker.

In a moment the entire fleet exhibited the flag of her holiness as the symbol of their new allegiance. This was a gratifying victory, as it procured for our cause more than sixty fully manned vessels of war and twenty-five thousand fletyemings.

Lyone was mistress of the seas!

"How came you to surrender at this juncture?" I inquired of the rear-admiral.

"Well, sir," he replied, "we have already lost more men and ships than if we had been engaged with an enemy similarly armed and having as many vessels as ourselves, and when the strange vessels came to your assistance we saw it was useless to prolong the fight. We saw that with your terrible weapons you were invincible. You can destroy us and we cannot destroy you, therefore I concluded, as rear-admiral of the fleet and successor to Admiral Jolar, who was killed in battle, that it was throwing life away to continue the fight. I saw, furthermore, that with you as the champion of the goddess her cause would succeed, and I wanted to be the first to render homage to her majesty."

"You have acted well," I replied, "and to reward your action, I now, in the name of her majesty, appoint and proclaim you rear-admiral of the fleet of Lyone, Queen of Atvatabar."

This announcement was received with frantic cheers by the sailors of both vessels.

Now that I was master of the sea, I intended to immediately extend my operations to the cause of the queen on land, and assuming the dignity of admiral, appointed Captain Wallace of the *Polar King* also rear-admiral of the fleet.

This announcements was received with the firing of guns and tremendous cheers.

"Rear-Admiral Wallace, Rear-Admiral Gerolio, and myself," I said to the sailors, "will determine the question of who will become the remaining high naval officers, and now that the battle is over, let us see that our wounded are properly cared for and all ships afloat put in proper repair."

It was a glorious victory!

All this time the two cruisers who so fortunately arrived in time to turn the tide of battle in our favor were rapidly approaching us, firing guns in honor of our victory. I acknowledged their arrival, as well as their valuable services, by having the royal fleet drawn up in double file, between which lay the *Polar King*, and ordering every vessel to give the strangers a salute of one hundred guns.

My anxiety to learn more of our allies was so great that I despatched two of my most active wing-jackets to the strange vessels to procure accurate information concerning them and their object in visiting the interior world. The wayleals returned with the information that the vessels were the United States ship of discovery *Mercury*, commanded by Captain Adams, and the English ship of discovery *Aurora Borealis*, commanded by Sir John Forbes. Both were fitted out by their respective governments to explore the interior world consequent on the report of Boatswain Dunbar and Seaman Henderson, the only survivors of the twelve men who left the *Polar King* when in the Polar Gulf. The respective commanders, officers and men of the incoming vessels were delighted to know that the *Polar King* was not only safe, but had discovered Atvatabar, and that its commander was at present king of the realm. This was the substance of the despatches sent me by Captain Adams and Commander Forbes, and addressed, "To Lexington White, Esq., Commander of the *Polar King*." Captain Adams stated that Boatswain Dunbar was on board his vessel as pilot, accompanied by Seaman Henderson.

Owing to the waterlogged condition of the *Polar King*, we could only wait the arrival of the vessels. When near at hand, a simultaneous salute of guns reverberated upon the sea, which must have been heard in all Atvatabar. Amid the smoke and noise of the roaring guns, steam launches had put off from the *Mercury* and *Aurora Borealis*, and in a very short time the commanders of both vessels stood upon the deck of the *Polar King*, accompanied by their respective officers. I embraced Captain Adams and Commander Forbes, and introduced the strangers to Rear-Admiral Wallace, Rear-Admiral Gerolio and staff, who were no less delighted and surprised than myself to receive visitors from the outer world. When the commanders reached the deck of the *Polar King* the cheers of the American and British sailors, mingled with the shouts of our fletyemings, made a soul-stirring scene.

In fact, I was already beginning to think the outer world a more or less mythical place, and thought the doctrine of reincarnation had an illustration or proof in myself. After all, the outer world really existed, and, strange as it seemed to the Atvatabarese, there was really an outer sun and live beings like themselves, only physically more vigorous.

It was necessary to set out at once for Kioram, as the *Polar King* was in a sinking condition.

Every man had been either killed or wounded. We made a total loss of sixty men, including the ten who left the ship in the Polar Gulf, thus making the entire company of the *Polar King* but fifty souls.

As for the ship, her plating was burst apart in many places and full of started bolts, caused by missiles of the enemy. The central compartment was filled with water, and the masts, sails, smoke-stack and hurricane-deck were practically destroyed.

Many of the guns were not struck once in the entire fight, and were ready for active service any moment. The terrorite battery was partially submerged, but still in good condition.

Captain Adams and Sir John Forbes both craved the honor of towing the *Polar King* into port, to which I willingly assented.

As admiral, I at once assumed command of the fleet, which I ordered to make sail for Kioram without delay. The fleet fell behind in good order, and followed the *Polar King*, bearing the victorious flag of the queen.

CHAPTER XLIV.

THE NEWS OF ATVATABAR IN THE OUTER WORLD.

THE kingdom of Atvatabar lay before us like a continent drawn upon a map, or, rather, upon the interior surface of a sphere or globe, everywhere visible to the naked eye. Its green forests, its impressive mountains, its rushing rivers, its white and many-colored cities, its wide-stretching shores, fringed with the foam of an azure sea, lay before the astonished eyes of our visitors.

When within a few miles of the city, Governor Ladalmir, accompanied by Captains Pra and Nototherboc, advanced to meet us in a large magnetic yacht, bearing the flag of Lyone. The governor hastened to inform us that, in view of our victory, the city of Kioram had declared its allegiance to the cause of Lyone, and invited myself and officers of the fleet, as well as our distinguished allies from the outer world, to a banquet in the fortress of Kioram. This news gave me great satisfaction, as the city would be a splendid base of military operations. The officers and seamen of the *Mercury* and *Aurora Borealis* created quite as great a sensation in the streets of Kioram as did the victorious sailors of the *Polar King.*

Landing on *terra firma*, Governor Ladalmir took the opportunity of showing our guests the beauty of his bockhockids, who formed a guard of honor to the fortress, where we were all royally received.

The two captains, together with their officers and sailors, were astonished at the multitude of strange objects shown them. Captain Adams would not remain satisfied until he was accoutred with a dynamo and a pair of magnic wings, with which all the sailors and soldiers of Atvatabar were supplied as part of their uniform. He was shown how the battery of metals gave motion to the dynamo, which in turn acted on the steel levers connected with the ribs of the wings. Although the worthy captain was of considerable weight, yet his astonishment at being able to skim through the air like a swallow was great. No sooner did he touch the button than all his preconceived notions of locomotion were destroyed, and he gasped with fear at his own prodigious motion. The two facts of unfailing movement of wings and exceptional buoyancy of body soon made him a fearless rider of the wind. He alighted on the earth with the greatest enthusiasm over the success of his experiment.

The magnic spear was another surprise for our guests. Sir John Forbes was astonished at my being able to fight the fletyemings so long, armed as they were by so potent a weapon of death. He would certainly recommend its use in the British army and navy on his return to England. Our allies were surprised at everything they saw, particularly at the rapid movements of the fletyemings or wing-jackets of the royal navy. They thought it an extraordinary thing the sailors should fly by magnic wings.

After the banquet Captain Adams, who was a fine type of an American seaman, bold, alert and courageous, gave us an account of how both the United States and England came to

send ships into the interior world. It appeared that the story of
Boatswain Dunbar first published in the New York papers, that
the *Polar King* had sailed down the Polar Gulf *en route* to an
interior world, had created a tremendous sensation on the outer
sphere, and all civilized nations immediately fitted out vessels of
discovery to follow up the *Polar King* and make discoveries for
the benefit of their respective governments. So far as any one
knew, only two vessels had succeeded in entering the interior
sphere.

The recital of Captain Adams was frequently interrupted by
Sir John Forbes, the British captain, a courageous officer, who
possessed all the stately dignity of his race. He stated that since
the discovery of America by Columbus no other event had
awakened such unbounded enthusiasm as the discovery of a
polar gulf and an interior world.

"I am most of all interested at present," said I, "in the story
of how Dunbar reached civilization again after parting with us. I
forgive you, Dunbar," I continued, addressing him, "for your
mutinous conduct, and now let us hear the story of your
adventures in the Polar Sea."

"Admiral," said Dunbar, "had we known the terrible
hardships we would have to endure in making our way home,
chiefly on foot and at the same time burdened with the boat,
we would never have left the ship. But you must thank me for
the presence of the two ships that are here to-day and for the
fame you already enjoy in the outer world."

"It's something tremendous," said Captain Adams.

"How did your geographers receive the news of the interior
world?" I inquired of Sir John Forbes.

"I need not say that the English geographers, in common
with the entire nation, were greatly excited at the news. The
Royal Geographical Society have already made you an honorary
member, and it was actually proposed at one of the meetings
that the government should proclaim a special holiday as a day
of rejoicing for so great a discovery. This would certainly have
been done but for the fact that the story rested entirely on the
testimony of two sailors, and that any public rejoicing should
be postponed until the story of the sailors would be verified by
a special expedition sent from England. Of course, many people
think that Dunbar's story is a fable or a hallucination that he
himself believes in. On the other hand, hundreds of professional

and amateur astronomers and geographers are proving by mathematics that the earth must be a hollow sphere, and the story of the open poles an entirely physical possibility."

"The people of the United States," said Captain Adams, "are almost unanimous in the belief that the interior world is a veritable reality, and it only requires a return of my ship to convince every one that Dunbar's story falls very short of the glorious reality."

"There is no man more famous to-day than Lexington White, Admiral of Atvatabar!" said Sir John Forbes.

"I thank you, gentlemen, for your kind words," said I; "and now for Dunbar's story."

"I think, admiral," said Captain Adams, "that if I were to read you the article containing Dunbar's story written by a special commissioner of the New York *Western Hemisphere*, who was the first to interview Dunbar at Sitka, on learning of his arrival there, it would be perhaps the best narration of his perilous adventures." As the captain spoke he drew a copy of the *Western Hemisphere* from his pocket.

"By all means," I replied, "let us hear what the press said about Dunbar and his adventures."

Thereupon Captain Adams read the New York *Western Hemisphere's* account of Dunbar's adventures, as follows:

"AN ASTOUNDING DISCOVERY!

"THE NORTH POLE FOUND TO BE AN ENORMOUS CAVERN,
LEADING TO A SUBTERRANEAN WORLD!
"THE EARTH PROVES TO BE A HOLLOW SHELL ONE
THOUSAND MILES IN THICKNESS, LIT BY AN INTERIOR SUN!
"OCEANS AND CONTINENTS, ISLANDS AND CITIES SPREAD UPON
THE ROOF OF THE INTERIOR SPHERE!
"BOATSWAIN DUNBAR AND SEAMAN HENDERSON, OF THE 'POLAR
KING,' HAVING DESERTED THE SHIP AS SHE WAS ENTERING
PLUTUSIA, HAVE ARRIVED AT SITKA, ALASKA,
IN A DESPERATE CONDITION, AND HAVE
BEEN INTERVIEWED BY A 'WESTERN
HEMISPHERE' COMMISSIONER.
"THEY SAY LEXINGTON WHITE, COMMANDER OF THE 'POLAR
KING,' IS AT PRESENT SAILING UNDERNEATH CANADA
ON AN INTERIOR SEA!

"TREMENDOUS POSSIBILITIES FOR SCIENCE AND COMMERCE!
"THE FABLED REALMS OF PLUTO NO LONGER A MYTH!
"GOLD! GOLD! BEYOND THE DREAMS OF MADNESS!

"The story of the discovery of Plutusia and the Polar Gulf, as
told by the two shipwrecked survivors of the mutineers of the
Polar King now at Sitka, Alaska, to the *Western Hemisphere*,
will form an epoch in the history of the world. The renown of
Columbus and Magellan is overshadowed by the glory of
Lexington White, a citizen of the United States, who fitted out
a ship for polar discovery, and, taking the command himself,
has unravelled the mystery of the North Pole, discovered the
Polar Gulf and the interior world.

"Having penetrated the Polar Gulf about three hundred
miles, and having discovered the interior sun, a fear seized on a
number of the sailors, among whom were Boatswain Dunbar
and his companion, Henderson, who are the only survivors of
twelve men who left the *Polar King* in an open boat to return
home again, and to whose safe arrival in Sitka the world is
indebted for news of the important discoveries that had been
made.

"Dunbar and Henderson arrived in Sitka in a very forlorn
condition, almost starved to death and utterly exhausted with
their terrible journey homeward. They seem to forget largely
the incidents of the journey outward in the *Polar King*, but have
a very clear recollection of their own individual experiences in
returning to civilization again. Dunbar, with his eleven
associates and the Esquimaux dogs, were no sooner cut adrift
from the *Polar King* than they began to realize their terrible
position. Borne on the breast of the immense tidal wave that
vibrated up and down the polar cavern, they were tossed
helplessly to and fro, now flung almost out of its mouth and
again sucked back into its midnight recesses. They floated for
days in the gigantic tunnel of water that threatened to collapse
any moment and overwhelm them. They would fain have
returned to the ship, but the breeze blowing out of the cavern
wafted them far from their comrades, and they therefore bent
all their energies to the task of getting home again. The light of
the polar summer that lit the mouth of the gulf was their guide
that led them back to the old familiar world.

"Happily for the adventurers, the direction of the wind

continued favorable to their voyage. They made about a
hundred miles a day, and in five days reached the edge of the
outer ocean. Here again the grandeur of the scene appalled
them. Let the reader imagine a little boat carrying twelve souls
out of that monstrous cavern five hundred miles in diameter.
Think of fifteen hundred miles of ocean forming the mouth of
the world that shone in the Arctic sunlight like molten silver
surrounding an abyss of darkness.

"Dunbar and his companions had no sooner emerged from
the gulf and seen once more the light of the sun — our own
sun — than they wept for joy. But again, when they thought of
the terrible barrier of ice they had to cross again they began to
wish they had remained with the *Polar King*. Thus man
fluctuates between this or that impulse, as he is moved.

" 'I say, captain,' said Walker, one of the men, 'don't you
think it about as safe to go back and find the ship as to run the
chance of being frozen to death on the ice?'

" 'Well,' said Dunbar, 'when we left the ship everybody knew
it was for good. Our shipmates have chosen their course, as we
chose ours, and it's too late to go back now. As likely as not she
may have struck a rock and has gone to the bottom by this
time.'

"As the boat cleared the cavern the sea fell down before
them, until at noonday the sun itself was visible, a joyful proof
that they had at last gained the normal surface of the earth
again.

"When three days out of the gulf, the weather grew suddenly
colder, and the sky became obscured with clouds, completely
hiding the sun from sight. A furious snow-storm overtook the
voyagers, who, benumbed with cold, wished they were only
back again under the hurricane-deck of the *Polar King*.
Fortunately, the wind blew steadily toward the Arctic Circle,
bringing them nearer home, but such was the anxiety and
suffering caused by insufficient protection from the inclement
climate that they cared not whither they drifted, so long as they
could keep alive.

"By the help of a little oil-stove they boiled their coffee
under a sail, which, spread horizontally above them, in some
measure kept the snow from burying them alive.

"The storm spent its fury in twenty-four hours, and when the
air grew clear again they were saluted with the sight of that

enormous ridge of ice through which the *Polar King* found a passage a month before. The ice was heaped up with the purest snow in places twenty feet in depth. Thousands of icy peaks and pinnacles, as far as the eye could reach, pierced the sky. Under other conditions the sight would have been sublime, but to men frozen and famished with insufficient food it was a scene of terror.

"The icy range was flanked by an ice-foot varying from thirty to sixty miles in width, and from four to fifty feet above the sea-level.

"Here was the problem that confronted Dunbar — he had to travel over at least thirty miles of icy splinters over an ice-foot whose surface was broken into every possible contortion of crystallization. There were mounds, hummocks, caverns, crevasses, ridges and gulfs of the hardest and oldest ice. Then when this barrier was crossed there was the icy backbone of the whole system, five hundred to a thousand feet in height, to be crossed, as there was no lane or opening to be discovered through so formidable a range of ice mountains. Even if he succeeded in crossing the same, there would certainly be an ice-foot of perhaps greater dimensions than the one before him to cross, and that might prove to be only a valley of ice leading to other and still more inaccessible cliffs to be surmounted.

" 'This is no place to die in,' said Dunbar, 'and so, boys, we've got to hustle if we ever expect to get home.'

" 'Ay, ay, sir,' said his companions, but when they reached the ice they found that having remained in a cramped position for a month in the boat had incapacitated them for walking.

"It was also found that Walker's feet and those of four other sailors had been frostbitten, and that they were totally unable to be of any service to themselves or the others.

"The outlook was mournful in the extreme. The only thing that cheered them was the constant sunlight, and even that consolation would depart in another month, and if in the mean time they did not get away from the ice, hunger and the awful desolation of a polar winter would terminate their existence.

"There was no chance of starting on their journey until they got accustomed to the use of their limbs, and so they built a hut of blocks of ice, which were solidly frozen together by a few buckets full of sea water thrown over them.

"The dogs were glad to get on the ice again, and scampered

We slowly dragged ourselves across the range of icy peaks.

about totally oblivious of the fact that the supply of pork was getting very low, and unless they got some fresh meat very soon they would be obliged to feed on each other.

"They remained a fortnight in their Arctic abode exercising themselves by cutting a passage in the ice. During this time four of the sailors died. Finally the remainder, packing everything into the boat, yoked the dogs thereto, and started in anything but hopeful spirits on their arduous journey.

"It was found that Walker had to be carried along, but he did not long continue a burden to his associates, for on the fourth day of the march he died, and was buried in the snow. It was a toilsome journey. Almost every foot of the way required to be hewn out of ice as hard as adamant.

"The dogs suffered greatly from insufficient food and tireless exertion. Several died from complete exhaustion, and were greedily devoured by their fellows.

"After desperate exertions, Dunbar and his company, now reduced to seven souls, gained the crest of the ice range and had the satisfaction of seeing open water not twenty miles away. It took some time to discover the best route for a descent, but at last they reached the level of the ice-foot beyond, and struck for open sea. A fortunate capture of several seals re-enforced their almost exhausted supply of provisions.

"Dunbar cared nothing about latitude or longitude or scientific information in such a desperate fight for life. It was a joyful moment when he and his companions launched their boat safe into the sea again after the incredible toil of dragging it forty miles across the splintered ice peaks and the terrible ice-foot north and south of the paleocrystic mountains.

"Dunbar hoisted his sail, abandoning the few dogs who yet remained alive, and with his unhappy companions steered for Behring Straight, first making for the coast of Alaska that faces the desolation of the Arctic seas.

"It would be impossible to describe the horrors of that lonely voyage. The terrible struggle with five hundred miles of ice-floes, with snow-storms that piled the snow high upon the voyagers, and the ferocious cold, proved too much for five of the seven sailors, and one by one the poor fellows died, and were thrown overboard.

"Only two men — Dunbar and a sailor named Henderson — emerged from the Arctic Sea, arriving in six months from the time they left the ship, in Sitka, Alaska."

TO BE   CONCLUDED

 *ROGNOSTICATIONS*

FOR our next issue, we're featuring a forgotten masterpiece by William Morris, the originator of the *genre* of modern heroic fantasy with such early novels as THE STORY OF THE GLITTERING PLAIN (1891), THE WOOD BEYOND THE WORLD (1895), THE WELL AT THE WORLD'S END (1896) and THE WATER OF THE WONDROUS ISLES (1897). We're sure you'll find "The Hollow Land" a treat rich and strange. Also, we hope to have a psychic chiller by the English master Algernon Blackwood, plus the conclusion of THE GODDESS OF ATVATABAR.

Our letter column, "Articulations," is off to a fine start this issue, thanks to all of you who took the time to write. Keep up the good work, and maybe next time we'll be able to report to you on some circulation and sales figures.

DM

RTICULATIONS

RESPONSE to the first issue of FORGOTTEN FANTASY has been most gratifying. I appreciate your comments and suggestions very much, and will try to respond to them as best I can. So here's the letter column I promised you; it's up to you to make it a lively and interesting one. Let's hear from you — I'll print as many letters as I have room for each issue. Write to me, Doug Menville, Nectar Press, Inc., 1521 N. Vine St., Hollywood, California, 90028.

Gentlemen:

I am delighted with the first issue of FORGOTTEN FANTASY and wish to congratulate you and Mr. Menville on your accomplishment. You supply a need.

The selection of the rare GODDESS OF ATVATABAR (complete with original illustrations) is noteworthy. The inclusion of the rare Doyle story is good indeed. Mr. Menville states the purpose and background of the publication in an admirable fashion in his editorial. Notes preceding stories are pleasantly informative. Illustrations are very good indeed.

Again, congratulations. Long may your creation flourish.

Best wishes,

Al Germeshausen
2720 Woodhaven Drive
Hollywood, California 90028

Many thanks for your kind words, Al. I intend to run original illustrations whenever they are available and interesting.

Dear Doug,

It's difficult to describe my impressions of FORGOTTEN FANTASY. First of all: Such a beautiful package! Hughes' cover is the most eyecatching I've seen in a long time. Original prints wouldn't be available, would they? Interior art is fully up to the cover's standards, and there was so much. Good art like that makes reading more fun.

I haven't read the serial, as I want to wait till I have it all. THE PARASITE was a good story, but a little too drawn out. "The Dead Smile" seemed more like a Gothic. It had supranormal elements, but the underlying situation was a mundane sin. I guessed the true relationship between Gabriel and Evelyn halfway through but discarded it in my mind, as it didn't fit into the story as a "fantasy" story.

It's a miracle my newsstand got your mag with distribution the way it is, but I'm certainly glad. The odds against you are high, as you well know, but I hope you make it. You've got my support.

Peace and Love,

Rick Stooker
1205 Logan St.
Alton, Illinois 62002

P.S.: Are you in the market for new stories?

Glad you liked Bill Hughes' cover, Rick. We think it's the best thing he's ever done. I intend to use as much interior art as possible, as I agree that it makes the reading more interesting. Sorry, but we're not in the market for new stories.

Al and Joe:

Sorry to be so long answering your request for comment on FORGOTTEN FANTASY.

First, the things I like.

1. My first suggestion before opening the mag was that the editor should establish personal relationship with readers. This you have done.

2. My second suggestion would have been that each story must have a detailed description of its history, etc. This you have also done. So much for that.

3. Your editor seems to be one of the old-timers, like me, and knows what he is about. Congrats on finding him.

4. Format, size, printing, illustrations, all first rate. No criticism at all here.

5. The title is inspired, very good. In fact, I think you have done a masterful bit of work . . . and work is the word for it.

Slight nit-picking: So many of these reprint fantasy-horror digests are on the stands, they sort of all blend into one another. Do you know what I mean? If you lined them all up, I would like the eye of the browser to be drawn to yours. Therefore, I would suggest you think about a bolder, more standout cover, that can be seen 20 feet away and is always the same, at least in title. Naked girls do not attract as they once did.

Also, Douglas Menville should use his full name, not just initials, in his comments. This may seem unimportant, but to a reader it cements a sort of *sharing* relationship. Believe me, I know.

Otherwise, FF is a beautiful job well done. Can you keep it up? All material in this first issue is unknown to me. That in itself takes a bit of doing.

I could suggest a lot of sources which I have not mentioned before. Have the Munsey copyrights or the FFM copyrights run out? How about ELECTRICAL EXPERIMENTER and SCIENCE AND INVENTION, early Gernsback mags which carried fantasy. At the turn of the century there was William Wallace Cook, after Verne and before Wells, who took off to the stars. Ask Menville. I have all of E.E. and most SCIENCE AND INVENTION.

Congratulations again, and if I can help in *any* way, call me.

> Daryl McAllister
> 204 N. Niagara
> Burbank, California 91505

Thanks for a most helpful letter, Daryl. We'll do our best to keep up the quality — and I think we may have quite a few more surprises in store for you. I'd like to stay away from magazine fiction as much as possible, as much of it is being and has been reprinted by other mags, although I will use an occasional magazine story or two. I am interested in William Wallace Cook, however, but have not been able to obtain any of the series. If any kind and trusting reader would like to lend them to me, I promise to take excruciatingly good care of them and return them promptly. I'd be particularly interested in seeing ADRIFT IN THE UNKNOWN or A ROUND TRIP TO THE YEAR 2000. Or — if anyone has them for sale, quote me a price.

Dear Mr. Menville:

Good heavens! Congratulations! I can't believe it! FORGOTTEN FANTASY is one of — if not the best — magazine I have ever picked up! It's mere coincidence that I decided to go uptown and look for a book — but instead, I found you! I think your magazine is beautiful — cool! It's too much. I love the fact that you are printing only or primarily — whichever — classic stories and novels. Your rare stories match your rare talent. When I picked up your magazine I knew I loved it at first sight. I hope — and know — that you will have great success, and I hope you also have stories by J. S. Le Fanu, Stoker, Derleth, Lovecraft and all the rest. Your artists are magnificent. I'm glad someone with your taste has formed this magazine. Keep up the tremendous work! Too much!

> Daniel Roberts
> Tiffin, Ohio 44883

That red glow you see in the West is not the sunset, Daniel — it's your editor blushing! If we are successful, it'll be because of readers such as yourself. I have stories by both Le Fanu and Stoker in mind for early issues.

Dear Mr. Menville:
This last Saturday night Bernie Zuber brought with him to our local Mythopoeic Society meeting a copy of issue one of FORGOTTEN FANTASY. I was very much impressed by it and should like to get a copy. Do any paperback sellers in Santa Barbara carry it?
This fall I will be starting a new course at Westmont on fantasy and science fiction. I should enjoy introducing your magazine to my class. I am, by the way, quite a fan of the nineteenth century fantasy writer, George MacDonald. Possibly some of his tales would fit into your FORGOTTEN series. Also, do you know Mervyn Peake's work? He has two (quite forgotten, I am sure) short stories, published in SCIENCE FANTASY No. 60 (1963): "Same Time, Same Place;" and No. 61 (1963): "Danse Macabre." I could send you copies, if you are interested.
Best of luck with FORGOTTEN FANTASY.

> Sincerely,

> Glenn Sadler,
> Assistant Professor of English
> Westmont College
> Santa Barbara, California 93103

By this time you should be finding FF regularly at newsstands in Santa Barbara. If not, back issues are available through the mail. I, too, am a fan of both MacDonald and Peake, but their works are currently being reprinted in Ballantine's Adult Fantasy series. I am familiar with the two stories you mention, but recall seeing at least one of them in a paperback anthology a few years back. I'm afraid they are both too recent for FF, but thanks for the offer. And good luck with your class.

Dear Mr. Menville:
Just yesterday I discovered your Vol. 1, No. 1 copy of FORGOTTEN

FANTASY in a small newsstand in Brevard, N.C. Since I was a regular reader of FAMOUS FANTASTIC MYSTERIES and FANTASTIC NOVELS (as well as A. MERRITT'S FANTASY), and still have many back copies of these magazines, I was extremely pleased to see at long last a worthy successor to these fine pulps.

Your initial selection of a novel, novelette, and short story (two of them by famous authors) was excellent and I hope that this standard will be maintained, since there is such an unmined treasure trove of "Forgotten Fantasy."

Also, let's hope for a substantial letters section since, as you rightly pointed out, this was an especially interesting part of FAMOUS FANTASTIC MYSTERIES.

I hope that the newsstands in Winston-Salem will also stock your magazine, and in the meantime I can only send you the best of wishes for complete success.

Very sincerely,

J.M. Johnson
2001 S. Main St., Apt. 206
Winston-Salem, North Carolina 27107

P.S.: Would you be able to provide the address of the publisher of the Robert A.W. Lowndes magazines mentioned by you on page 6?

Gladly. Write to: Health Knowledge, Inc., 140 Fifth Ave., New York, N.Y. 10011

Dear Sirs,

Please accept this letter as a vote for the success of your magazine, FORGOTTEN FANTASY. I'm sure it will help to fill the void left by FFM and FN by publishing the wonderful old masterpieces that some of us have only read about.

As a suggestion, could you publish some of Merritt's shorts, such as "The Fox Woman," and THE BLACK WHEEL; also some of Haggard's scarcer novels.

I hope that everyone who truly enjoys this type of literature will support your magazine.

Yours truly,

John H. Dennis
511 Orlando Drive
Robinson, Illinois 62454

Unfortunately, the Merritt stories you mention are unavailable to us at this time, but I do intend to run some Haggard in the future.

Doug—

I bought your magazine today and I'd like to congratulate you on it. The story by Doyle is one of the best fantasy stories I've read in a long time.

My only complaint on the zine was the type size; can't you make it a little smaller?

You've suggested a letter column; how about an article in each issue about one of the authors or about some facet of the fantasy field? I also think that instead of printing the cover painting on both the front and back, perhaps you should just have printing on the front and the painting on the back. I don't really like your logo much either.

But to get away from these petty complaints, your zine looks to be the most exciting and interesting on the market. I also hope that you keep publishing just three or four stories an issue. Maybe you should try two. The problem with most reprint mags on the market is that they seem to feel that to be competitive with major "new story" magazines they have to publish six, seven, eight stories an issue.

Most of the longer stories are the better ones; this is true of the early stories particularly. On closing, I would just like to congratulate you on a splendid magazine.

> Tony Breen
> Box 242
> Groton, Massachusetts 01450

I intend to keep pretty much to the present format, Tony, unless a majority of readers indicate a preference for change. I'll keep your other suggestions in mind also, as the magazine evolves.

Dear Mr. Menville:

In your editorial in the (your) new magazine I picked up today, you invited comments, so I am taking you at your word.

First of all, let me wish you the greatest success in the world in this new venture and hope you can make it GO, GO, GO. You see, I, too, was a fan of Mary Gnaedinger and an avid supporter of FANTASTIC NOVELS and FAMOUS FANTASTIC MYSTERIES. You have one handicap, not so evident in the FFM/FN days. Many of the old Munsey fans are dead and gone, and the present day breed of SF readers in many cases have never heard of the old authors and the old classic story titles, so it leaves them cold. There are a few readers that are against reprints in any form, so you have their resistance to overcome. I admit that I am prejudiced in favor of the old school of authors who emphasized fantasy, fantastic adventure, the weird, the supernatural, and good old swashbuckling action, lost races, and a generous helping of romance and love element. Space operas still leave me cold in spite of the fact that we have been to the moon.

Miss Gnaedinger did two things that you could do well to emulate. She planned her magazines to care for the long serial stories (book length), and she used modern art work by Virgil Finlay and others. The old stereotype illustrations were discarded entirely. Perhaps they could be added at the back of the magazine for curiosity, nothing more. No one wants to visualize his hero in a derby hat, and with a soup-strainer such as worn by Theodore Roosevelt/Howard Taft, etc. No one wants to see the heroine in a high bodice, corset, ankle-length dresses, button shoes, etc. Illustrations must be sexy in the modern vein.

I am not sure from your editorial just where you plan to find your "old classics," but I am sure you realize that most of the really good and most wanted stories still reside in the files of ARGOSY, ALLSTORY WEEKLY, and CAVALIER. Miss Gnaedinger, in FFM/FN, only got about 50% of the old stories out into the light of day. Donald Wollheim at Ace has added some more titles by paperback, but several dozen stories are still "buried" in the stacks and threatened with oblivion. Consider these: Charles B. Stilson: A MAN NAMED JONES, LAND OF THE SHADOW PEOPLE (sequal to JONES); Garret Smith: AFTER A MILLION YEARS, TREASURES OF TANTALUS, CLOUD HAWK, THE GIRL IN THE MOON, plus many fine short stories; Homer Eon Flint: THE PLANETEER, KING OF CONSERVE ISLAND, THE Nth MAN, THE MAN IN THE MOON, OUT OF THE MOON; George Allan England: THE EMPIRE IN THE AIR, THE FATAL GIFT; Francis Stevens: AVALON, LABYRINTH, NIGHTMARE; Garret P. Serviss: A COLUMBUS OF SPACE; Ralph Milne Farley: THE RADIO MENACE, THE RADIO PIRATES, THE RADIO GUN RUNNERS, THE RADIO WAR, THE IMMORTALS; plus a host of other stories by such authors as Ray Cummings, Victor Rousseau, Perly Poore Sheehan, Murray Leinster, Philip M. Fisher, Jr., and many others. You see, I am an ARGOSY collector and have many of these stories in their original form, but feel very sorry for those SF readers who have never had a chance to read them. Most of them are far better than the pap we are being dished out today. To the best of my knowledge, the stories listed above have never been reprinted in the USA in any form.

You may be faced with some copyright problems, but if you can locate the old authors or their heirs, you can deal with them directly and bypass the first magazine copyright. Many of the stories were not renewed after the first 28 years and are already in public domain. Others that got renewed are now coming up to their second 28-year period, and will soon pass the magic number of 56 years and enter public domain. This should help a lot. Another item there that Mary Gnaedinger had the advantage over you: She was working for the company that owned the original copyrights, which in many cases permitted unlimited reprints. An outsider is not so lucky.

Let's hope that you can succeed where others have failed, and those long-lost Munsey classics can again see the light of day. All the fans of this new generation should be eternally grateful.

Kindest regards,

Charles W. Wolfe
716 Cardenas Dr. NE
Albuquerque, New Mexico 87108

As I mentioned earlier in this column, I had originally planned to use primarily material from books, with only a few magazine stories now and then, since I feel that early book fantasy has been even more neglected than the Munsey classics. However, if enough readers want Munsey material, I shall certainly look into the possibility of reprinting some of the stories you mention. One problem is that I do not have access to the magazines myself, nor the time and resources to try and track them down through the mail. How about this, readers?

Dear Doug:

Just a note to thank you for the copy of the first edition of FORGOTTEN FANTASY. The lineup looks good, but, as you can guess, I am about four months behind in my reading ... and have, before me stacked up to the sky, about 20 novels, books of stories, essays, poems by friends who need criticism ... so I haven't had a chance to read any of the stories in your magazine ... but they all look like great fun.

As for your cover painting? I don't know what sells magazines any more. I am tired of naked ladies gesturing at maelstroms, but obviously I grow old, and just as obviously others find these sad ladies worthy of attention. I don't recall that they ever really sold me that much on the old WEIRD TALES, even when fetchingly done by Finlay. Anyway, my Ma always used to rip the jackets off the magazines when she found them, so good old teen-age Ray wouldn't be corrupted.

Sorry I haven't more to offer in criticism or help right now, but I am working for Disney's Robot Factory in Glendale, creating the Monsanto Theatre at Disney World, Florida! Grand fun, working with robots, lights, films, etc., etc!

Good luck with the magazine.

Best,

Ray Bradbury
Los Angeles, California

Sorry you didn't dig our maelstrom-gesturing miss, Ray; how does Bill's cover for this issue strike you? Best of luck at the Robot Factory!

Gentlemen:

Just a few brief remarks on the first issue of FORGOTTEN FANTASY.

I managed to get a page and a half into THE GODDESS OF ATVATABAR before giving up in disgust. William Bradshaw couldn't have been a good writer in his own day, and today he simply stinks. Not only does he lack any sort of sense for language (which was a common failure of writers of his era), but he has no sense of style (which was *not* common in those days). He is also woefully weak on background and displays a fondness, intentional or otherwise, for malapropisms and created words. "Splot," for instance, unless that's a mis-spelling. As far as I'm concerned, the less we see of Mr. Bradshaw, the better. To quote Willy Ley on a similar subject: "There is good old science fiction, but most of it, alas, is simply old."

On the other hand, F. Marion Crawford's "The Dead Smile" is extremely good. The story was basically slight, but it was as well told as any of Lovecraft's tales. Crawford not only had style, but he observed keenly and put what he observed into his work. The man may be a forgotten fantasist today, but if all his stories are that good, he certainly deserves to be revived. As long as you print stories like that, you'll have at least one faithful reader.

In the same vein, please don't fall into the same trap as the late, unlamented COVEN 13. I'm aware it's a risky business for an independent publisher to start a new magazine, but I'm firmly convinced the reason COVEN 13 failed was the extremely low quality of the stories they published. I bought the first issue of the magazine in high hopes — only to have them dashed after the first few pages. I purchased one other issue because they had a good lead story, but I found out the rest of the magazine was as bad as their first issue. I'd hate to see you go the same way. With all the really fine fantasy that's been published over the last 75 years or so, I'm sure you can find enough good-to-excellent material to fill your issues.

Sincerely,

Rick Cook
4845 E. Earll Dr.
Phoenix, Arizona 85018

We'll give it a helluva try, Rick. Don't write off COVEN 13 too soon — it's been sold to a new publisher, and an all-new editorial staff intends to bring out another issue soon (by the time you read this, it may already be out) with material by Lovecraft, Howard, Petaja, and others. Incidentally, "splot" was a typo — sorry about that.

www.ingramcontent.com/pod-product-compliance
Lightning Source LLC
Chambersburg PA
CBHW050802250626
47155CB00005B/2172